Books by Lucas McWilliams

Savage Summer
Eternal Hunt
Eternal Lies

**Middle age Books by father-daughter
team Lucas and Sophia McWilliams**

Wielders #1 The Journey Begins
Wielders #2 First Battle
Wielders #3 The Hunter
Wielders #4 Silver Town Championship
Wielders #5 Lost Friend

And look for more coming out soon!

www.Wielders.us
www.LucasMcWilliams.com

Eternal Hunt
By Lucas McWilliams

Copyright © 2013 Lucas McWilliams
Layout by Lucas McWilliams

ISBN# 978-1-939037-07-7

www.Wielders.us
www.LucasMcWilliams.com

Coval Press
Lancaster, KY

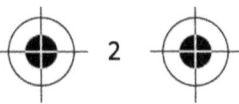

For my wife and three wonderful girls who bring a smile to my lips each day.

Special thanks to the dedicated few that really went above and beyond in helping me complete this process. Joan, Larry & Lucas's lovely wife Laura.

And thank you, dear reader!

Table of Content

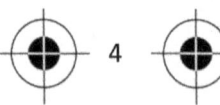

Eternal Hunt
By Lucas McWilliams

Chapter 1:
Bear Ridge

I can't believe it's taken six weeks for us to get a break in the weather long enough to search for Caleb. He was leading six hunters into the back woods to go moose hunting when their pilot sent a distress call declaring an emergency and that they were going to crash. That was the final message received from Caleb's group. Their last known location was just north of Bear Ridge. Our rescue party is heading to an old hunter's cabin in that area, hoping that they holed up in it for shelter.

Caleb and I have been coming to Alaska for years, working as big game hunting guides. We grew up together and are cousins, but are closer than brothers. We are both full-blooded Seneca Indians from a small reservation in southern New York State. Caleb is a very capable guide and hunter, but six weeks of blizzard in the Alaskan wilderness would be

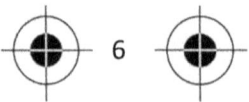

hard for anyone to survive. I just hope we find him alive.

My father is furious with me for not returning to college for my last semester. I was looking forward to graduating but I had to stay and help Caleb by assisting with the search. We came up to Alaska over spring break for a few guide jobs. Caleb's plane went down and I didn't even know about it until I got back from my hunt five days later. My group was farther to the south and didn't get the bad storms that Caleb had up north.

I'm with a six-man rescue team flying up in a chopper to the Bear Ridge area. There was supposed to be an EMT on the chopper named Danny but he got sick at the last minute. I look around the chopper at the members of the rescue party. Enuk is a local Inuit Indian and a friend of mine. He is a hunting guide, like Caleb and me. Enuk is in his late thirties and has been hunting since he was knee high to a caribou. Enuk is a tall, rangy man with deep-set brown eyes and a slight scar across one cheek. He got the scar hunting a bull moose in his teens. He went to skin the big bull after he had shot it and, well, it was not quite dead.

Then, there is Liz and Robert. They are a local couple who volunteered to help. Liz is involved in marketing trips to Alaska and is one of those super-hot outdoorsy types. She has long blond hair and round china blue eyes. She would look like a china doll if it weren't for her athletic build and generous breasts. Robert is a bank manager who tries to keep up with Liz. He has dark hair and eyes, wears wire-rimmed glasses and preppy outdoor wear. I wonder if he has used any of his gear before today? He is about ten years older than Liz and I bet his money has something to do with her hanging around. I know we waited to head out until Saturday morning so they could come along. I kind of resent them for making us wait but am glad to have more help in the search. The weather didn't really clear till Friday afternoon so we didn't lose that much time.

We have a young park ranger in charge of our group. He is sitting across from me. His name is Todd and I've known him for a while. He is a little too overconfident for my taste. He is just one of those dicks who thinks he can lick the world. He doesn't believe we'll find any survivors and is along just because it's part of his job. Like I said, he's kind of an ass. Todd is clean cut, military style. Kind of buff, not handsome, not ugly, just average looks.

The last member of our group is the bush pilot, old Buck. Buck is in his sixties but still flies all the time. He grew up in Alaska and knows this area like the back of his hand. Buck constantly chews tobacco and spits anywhere he damn well pleases.

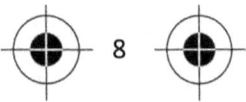

Then there is me, Logan Longstride. I've been hunting up here in Alaska since I was ten. Caleb and I went on many a trip with my father and grandfather up into the wilderness of Canada and Alaska. They would teach us the old ways of the Seneca. We learned how to walk without sound, track animals, hunt at night with a torch, how to skin and dress animals and how to survive in the wild. Every summer we would spend a couple months wandering in the wilderness, practicing and living the old ways. The last few years Caleb and I've been taking jobs leading hunters to the far wilderness and helping them get the trophies they so dearly want. The pay has been great and we like the work. That was until Caleb got lost.

The rescue team brought enough supplies to stay out in the wild for four days. After that, we'll have to be resupplied. Frankly, if Caleb is not at the hunter's cabin up by Bear Ridge, we probably won't ever find him. The plane that went down is most likely covered over by several feet of snow and will not be discovered till late summer, if at all. I just hope they radioed their position correctly when they were going down and Caleb remembered that old hunting cabin.

"How deep do you think the snow is down there?" Liz asks, looking out the window of the helicopter.

No one seems to want to answer so I offer my opinion. "Pretty deep, a couple feet at least. The main thing you have to watch for is crossing over a ravine or wash. Those areas can be much deeper and the snow can be unstable. You don't want to disappear under the snow in one of those places. Just wear your snowshoes, keep up with us and you should be ok."

She looks at me and I know she is intrigued by what she sees. I've always been told I'm a handsome man. I start braiding my long black hair so it will be out of the way for the trek through the wild. There should not be that many trees in the immediate area but the search could extend into the brush or forest. Way up north there aren't many trees at all but we are not that far north. I hope that we can stick to the lower valleys where the thaw should be hitting soon.

Liz watches me braid my hair. She seems entranced by it. I can tell Robert doesn't like her interest in me one bit, but I don't care what he thinks.

"You might want to braid or cover your hair, miss. I can tell you from experience that it's not pleasant to have your hair ripped out by a tree branch," I offer, as I finish up my own hair. I whip my head to throw the braid behind my head and smile at Liz.

Liz smiles at me, takes out a hat and stuffs her beautiful blond locks up inside it. I guess I'm kind of an jerk to be flirting with another man's woman when

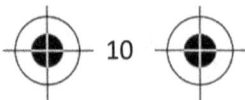

my cousin might be dead somewhere below. Liz is only Robert's woman as long as she wants to be. My dad has learned that the hard way, with my mom leaving and all.

"We're almost there, get your gear ready," Buck orders as he spits a particularly juicy wad of tobacco into his spittoon bucket.

"Remember the first rule is everyone stays together. We don't need any heroes getting themselves lost," Todd says, mostly looking at me.

I bet I know this area better than he does. He sits behind a desk more than he goes out in the wild. I know how Caleb thinks. If anyone can find him, it will be me.

The chopper puts down in a valley about four miles from the cabin up on Bear Ridge. I wish we could have gotten closer but the snow is too deep and there are few clearings to land in this area. I argued that we should have gone down on ropes next to the cabin but Todd didn't go for it. He didn't think everyone could make it and he insists we all stay together. Enuk and I could have easily gone down the ropes and checked out the cabin in a matter of minutes.

We unload our packs and the extra gear. Buck takes the chopper back up to do a couple of sweeps of the area before he heads back to town. He will return in four days, or before if we call him. Todd has a satellite phone and there is a long-range radio with our equipment.

We gear up and head off to the cabin. I instinctually take the lead but Todd wants to be the big man. "Hold up there, Logan, I'll take point," Todd commands.

I stop and sweep my arm for him to get his ass up here then. Enuk shakes his head at me and I know that he thinks Todd is about as useful as a lame sled dog.

After about a mile, Liz moves a little closer to me with Robert right on her heels. "Is it much further?" she asks.

"Yeah, further than we have already come. Trudging through snow wears on you after a while," I say, starting to feel a little burn in my own calves.

"One of the lost group was a friend of yours?" she asks, trying to make conversation.

"Caleb, my cousin, was their guide. I'm up here to find him."

"I've never been out this far before or seen so much snow this low down the mountains."

"It has been one hell of a spring. The storms would just not let up," I agree, looking at the clouds in the distance hoping they are not bringing more snow.

"Are the bears up yet? I see you men are carrying rifles," Liz wonders, looking around as if a bear might pop out of the snow anytime.

"They should be getting up about now. They will be hungry and moving down the mountains. I always carry a gun in the wild. It's pretty much a habit. I wouldn't worry about bears, they are scared of people," I reassure her.

We take a break and I can see Liz and Robert do not have their snowshoes tied right. I wander over to them and kneel down in front of Liz taking her foot in my hands.

Liz looks surprised but also raises her eyebrow curiously. Robert's expression sours and his eyes fling daggers at me for touching his property. "Now look here, what are you doing?" He demands getting to his feet.

"Your snowshoes are on wrong. Just trying to help," I reply as I untie and redo Liz's snowshoe. My hand moves up her calf and I glance up at Liz. She has a corner of her lip in her teeth and is holding her breath. I can tell she very much likes my attention. I take my time doing her other snowshoe and make sure to rub her leg a few times before I'm done.

"How does that feel, Liz?" I smile, still kneeling in front of her.

"Much better. Thanks, Logan," she smiles back at me, her blue eyes twinkling.

"You want me to help you with your snowshoes?" I ask Robert.

"I can manage," he insists, desperately trying to redo his snowshoe's ties. I'm pretty sure he just made things worse but he's not about to admit that he needs my help. A man that is too proud to accept help is not much of a man in my book.

Todd gets everyone up and we head out. Enuk is behind Todd watching his rookie mistakes. I'm bringing up the rear now making sure everyone keeps up.

I hear Enuk yell, "That way is not safe, we should go around."

I move up a bit so I can get a better look. Todd ignores Enuk and heads out over a ravine filled with snow. Enuk does not follow and just watches. Todd makes it most of the way across then in a swoosh he disappears below the snow. "Ahhh..., get me out of here," Todd screams.

"Rookie, I believe I talked about ravines covered in snow on the chopper," I comment, as I walk past Liz and Robert.

Enuk and I get a rope and throw it down to Todd making sure not to get out on the unstable snow ourselves. We are pulling Todd out of the snow when Liz screams from behind us. "Ahh..."

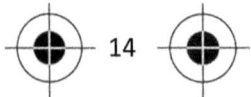

Enuk and I let Todd slip back down in the hole a little, as we are startled by Liz's scream. We pull Todd out of the hole and I head over to Liz.

Robert and Liz are standing where I left them. Liz's arm is raised up and her finger is out as if pointing at something. I follow her finger but see only a small patch of trees. It does look like the snow has been disturbed by something. I can't tell if it was an animal or a human. I take hold of Liz's shoulder and look into her eyes.

She is in shock, her eyes glazed and filled with tears of fear. "What did you see Liz?"

She comes out of her trance and falls into my arms, hugging me. "It was a…man, I think. He was covered in blood and naked. We have to leave, Logan. Please, take me away from this awful place?" she begs, starting to shake and cry uncontrollably.

I try to get her calmed down enough to hand her off to Robert. It takes Robert pulling and me pushing to pry Liz off me. I see that Todd is getting back to his feet so I motion for Enuk to come over to me. Then together we walk over to where Liz pointed. I unsling my rifle and Enuk does the same.

"Liz said she saw a bloody naked man over here by this stand of trees." He nods and we go into hunting mode. We watch, listen, smell and even taste the air as we move slowly forward. We instinctively move away from one another so we can catch any prey between us. There is an unnatural silence in the air. I know that earlier I had heard birds and the wind but now there is nothing but an eerie stillness. I don't like it and I can tell Enuk feels the same way. Something is definitely out of place here.

We walk cautiously up to the disturbed area of snow. There is a strange musky smell of death, like the air around a grave. I motion for Enuk to come over as I study the tracks of whatever Liz saw. There are definitely a couple of tracks and some drops of blood so something or someone has been here recently. I see human footprints but they are unlike any I have ever seen. The foot is certainly bare because I can make out each toe. However, the toes seem to have claws on them. They look like those I would see in a bear track. I point this out to Enuk and he stands next to me as perplexed as I.

A naked man would die out here in these subzero temperatures in a matter of minutes. Something is very wrong here.

"Let's track it," I suggest, following the tracks.

"This is bad medicine, Logan. I think we should leave it be. Whatever made these tracks is not natural," Enuk says as he takes out his medicine bag and offers up a small prayer.

"Come on guys, the cabin is this way," Todd yells from below.

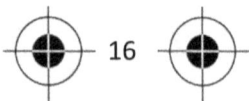 16

I take a few more steps and then head back to the others. I know Enuk is freaked out and that worries me as much as those strange tracks. Enuk is a great hunter who is full of courage. Anything able to affect him like that worries me. I decide to walk with my rifle in my hand from now on. I would like to know what we are facing and consider slipping off alone to follow the tracks. But I know this is a bad idea, so I go back to the group.

Liz is still shaken up but is glad to be moving once again. It's mid-morning and we should be at the cabin by noon. Buck flies over us in the copter waving, heading back to home base.

I walk up to Enuk. "What do you think left that track?" I ask.

"I can only think of our legends of the cursed men who have gone against our ancient laws. I can think of no animal or man that could leave such a track," Enuk says, looking around with concern in his eyes. Normally, he would not show his fear and this bothers me more than the tracks. Enuk is a brave hunter, stoic and strong.

I think about what Enuk said and a shiver runs down my spine. I know the legends of my tribe better than most. There are stories of cursed men that become part beast. I'm not as much a believer as I was when I was younger, but something sure made those tracks and I can't explain them or that weird musky smell of death.

We come over a ridge and spot the cabin. The snow is up to the roof all around the cabin except for the front where the door is. Someone or something has clearly been going in and out of the cabin. We make our way down to the cabin.

I notice some of those same clawed tracks and point them out to Enuk. He stops and looks all around with his rifle ready. I can smell the same musky smell of death in the air as well. Whatever Liz saw has been here recently.

Todd goes in the cabin and immediately comes right back out, vomiting. He bends over and lets his breakfast splatter on the snow.

"Enuk you watch out here, while I take a look," I suggest.

Enuk nods and scans the area. I walk up to the cabin and can smell death coming from within mixed with that strange musky smell of the grave. I move to the threshold and scan the two-room cabin. The smell of death is almost overwhelming. I enter the cabin and find a pile of bones with little bits of flesh clinging to them. The bones are human and appear to have been gnawed upon. The pile is large and I think made up of more than one person. I pick up one of the bones and take it over to the light so I can see it better.

It's definitely human and has been chewed on. I think I know by what but I want to hear what Enuk thinks.

"Enuk, take a look at this."

Enuk examines the bone. His face is pale and I know my initial thoughts were correct.

"Cannibal?" I ask.

"Does your tribe have the story of the Wendigo?" Enuk asks me as he looks all around.

"Yes, do you think that is what did this?" I ask, not really wanting to know the answer.

"It fits. A man that eats the flesh of another is cursed to become a Wendigo. Cursed to always crave the flesh of man but never be satisfied," Enuk stares off as his thoughts wander to thoughts best not dwelled upon.

Todd is getting a hold of himself. Liz and Robert are staying back, but I can tell they know something bad happened here.

"How the hell did a bear get in there?" Todd demands, still spitting out the last of his breakfast and wiping his mouth with the back of his glove.

"It was not a bear," Enuk insists.

"Then what was it, Eskimo man?"

"It was a man. They were starving and one or more of them decided to eat the others. Someone in that party became a cannibal," Enuk reveals, looking Todd in the eye with a penetrating stare. Todd backs up slightly, looking around nervously.

Liz freaks out at this statement and nearly starts vomiting. Robert does what he can to comfort her.

"Are you fucking crazy? People don't eat people. It was just a damn bear," Todd yells, not dealing with the situation very well.

Just then, I see movement behind Todd. I bring my gun up as it attacks Todd. The beast slices into Todd from the back with razor sharp talons. Blood splatters the pure white snow where Todd is standing. "Ahhh..." Todd screams. In seconds, the beast drags Todd off into a stand of trees.

"BANG...BANG," Enuk's rifle reports. I know he hit the thing, but it didn't even seem to notice.

It must have been a Wendigo. It was a naked man with talons for fingernails and toenails. It's skin was stretched tight over it's bones. It was emaciated like nothing I've ever seen. It's naked skin was the ash grey of death, like a walking corpse. Its eyes were black as night and sunken deep into the sockets. It was as if it was a risen gaunt skeleton, fresh from the earth. It smelled strongly of a musky odor of the grave, of death and corruption. It's lips were tattered and bloody. It's body was unclean and splattered with the blood of its victims. It let out a chilling howl like the wind rushing through a ravine that shot a shiver up my spine. It's head was still covered in long tangled hair. The hair was all black except for a white patch on the top. Right then, I knew who it had been when it was still a man. Caleb was born with a white patch of hair just like this creature. I was too startled by the realization that it was Caleb to even get a shot off.

"Caleb...Caleb...What have you done?" I scream as I drop to my knees, pounding my fist on the snow.

Recognition flashes across Enuk's face and I know that he also realizes that the thing was once Caleb, our companion. Enuk comes over to me as I'm coming out of my rant.

"We have to leave this cursed place," Enuk demands, pulling me to my feet.

I know he speaks the truth. I'm not even sure we can kill Caleb. Damn, I mean the Wendigo. My cousin Caleb is already dead. I have to keep telling myself that. Caleb is dead. What we saw was a Wendigo that has taken over Caleb's dead body. I know the only way that could have happened is if Caleb became a cannibal, but I try to push those thoughts out of my head.

Liz is in a crumpled heap on the ground. She totally lost it when the Wendigo took Todd. Damn, Todd had the satellite phone on him. Well, at least we have the radio in one of these packs.

"Enuk, let's find the radio and get Buck back here ASAP," I suggest, starting to look for the radio myself.

"What the hell was that? It just came and took Todd..." Robert stammers.

"It doesn't matter. Let's get the radio so we can all get out of here," I say, still digging through the piles of gear.

"All of us…all of us but Todd you mean. That…that thing…was a…man," Robert stammers pointing to where it took Todd with a shaking finger.

"It used to be a man…" I correct, silently cursing under my breath because I cannot find the damn radio.

"Enuk, have you seen the radio?" I ask.

"You don't think we left it on the chopper or was Todd maybe carrying it?" Enuk says, starting to rummage through the other packs.

I head over to Robert and Liz. I remove Liz's pack as she is crying and not about to take it off herself. The radio is not there. I'm about to go for Robert's pack when he points behind me. I watch as his face fills with terror.

I swirl around in time to see the naked rail thin body of Caleb rush into sight. It's heading right at Enuk. I fire and yell at the same time. "BANG!…Enuk, look out!…BANG!"

Enuk narrowly dodges the Wendigo. Robert takes off, which is probably what saves Enuk. The Wendigo sees Robert and races off after him. Enuk and I fire into the gaunt skeleton form of the Wendigo. "BANG…BANG…BANG."

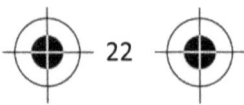 22

It moves so fast, it seems to leave no tracks upon the snow. It glides over the snow as if it's carried by the wind and doesn't even weigh enough to sink into the snow. It swerves in a zig zag as it closes in on Robert. All I can do is shoot at it over and over. I know I missed a couple times but most of my shots hit home. The Wendigo hardly notices. Caleb, my blood brother, I fear we may be the death of one another.

The Wendigo catches up to Robert and carries him off. We can hear Robert scream for a couple minutes as the Wendigo takes him farther and farther away. Then abruptly the screams stop and I'm sure Robert is dead. I feel strangely calm even though I know I could die at any moment.

Liz is in total shock, crumpled into a lump on the snow. I wish I could do more for her but we need to figure out what to do to save us all. The radio is not here so either it was on Todd or Robert or we left it on the chopper. I know Todd had a sat phone, so finding that is probably our best bet.

"Enuk, do you know how to fight a Wendigo?" I ask, trying to remember all I can of the stories I was told as a boy.

"Fire would probably be the best we could do with what we have," he says.

"The cabin is a slaughter house but it's our only real shelter from that thing. Go in and try to start a fire. I'll get Liz."

Enuk nods and goes in the cabin. I hear a lot of scraping from inside and I figure he is clearing out the bones. I go over to Liz and try to get her to her feet. She is pretty much dead weight in her present condition so I have to carry her. I put Liz in a corner of the cabin. I secure the door as best I can with the bolt and take stock of our supplies. It looks like we have enough wood for a day, maybe two if we burn what little furniture there is. I help get all the scattered bones into the smaller room and close the door. The place stinks of death but that cannot be helped. It's better than the alternative.

Enuk gets a good fire going and we look to the door. We use the table and chairs to block and reinforce it. Enuk starts working on a couple of torches and puts the end of his long hunting knife at the edge of the fire so the tip will be red hot. I put the metal poker in the fire and set my long bowie knife in the fire as well. We can use every little edge at this point.

"I figure the closest civilization is Goose Creek to the southwest, does that sound right?" I ask Enuk, as we work.

"That should be the closest, but it's over fifty miles."

"It would be a hard trip under regular conditions, but with that thing out there and Liz, like she is, I

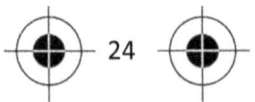

don't see how we could make it," I say, looking at Liz huddled in the corner.

"We better just hold up here till Buck gets back," Enuk agrees.

Buck won't be back for four days and three full nights with that thing hunting us all the while. This is not going to be easy. We had better get some rest. Tomorrow we can venture out for more firewood. I move Liz closer to the fire and stroke her back until she goes to sleep. I lie next to her and try to get some sleep even though it's early. We may be up the rest of the night if the Wendigo comes back.

Chapter 2: Trapped

I wake a few times during the night to put sticks on the dying fire. Enuk sleeps next to the door so he will wake if the Wendigo tries to get in. The third time I wake up, I'm startled to see Liz looking at me. Her eyes are alive and not dulled with shock any longer. She leans into me kissing my lips. I return her kiss and her passion becomes unleashed. Her tongue darts around my mouth frantically.

She grabs my hand and thrusts it between her legs. She helps me unbutton her jeans and pushes my hand under her panties. "Are you sure…" I mutter.

"I need something real right now. Please make me forget, Logan," she begs, her fingers pushing mine into her.

Who am I to turn down a woman's desires? I dip my fingers into her like a hungry bear desperate for honey. Whispers of pleasure escape her lips as I push her over the edge. She quivers in my arms as the waves of orgasm take her. "Again…again" is all she can manage to say. I do as I'm bid and soon she is wracked by another wave of pleasure. She is now spent and cuddles up to me. I watch as sleep takes her once again.

I fantasized about being with Liz but not like this. Not as a distraction to keep her sane in the face of nearly certain death. All she wanted was pleasure with no concern for my needs. Despite my bitching, I'm glad Liz is lying in my arms.

The next morning we have some hard biscuits, jam and a couple slices of cheese. Our water is low so we'll need to get some snow to melt. The firewood is also getting low so we are going to have to go outside. All we can see of the outside is from cracks around the door. The couple of windows of the cabin are totally covered with snow.

"I saw some wood about a hundred feet to the right of the cabin, over by the stand of trees," I comment to Enuk.

He nods. "Yes, I saw some downed limbs over there. We will need to make a few trips to get enough wood. You want to carry wood or be the lookout?" Enuk asks.

"As I recall, you are the better shot, not that guns have slowed the Wendigo down much. I'll get the firewood, while you cover me. I think we should take a torch with us, just in case."

"Liz, can you fill all the pots and cups full of snow? You can stay close to the door and just make a couple of trips," I ask, not sure she is up to it.

"I'll try," she mutters. I can tell she is really scared but she picks up a pot in each hand and gets ready to go.

Enuk and I get our knives and guns ready. We leave the poker in the fire. Enuk lights a torch and we head outside. The day is clear and the sun feels good on my face even though it's below freezing. The best part about going outside is the clean air. The stench in the cabin only got worse, when the heat from the fire thawed some of the rotten flesh.

I head straight for the firewood, counting on Enuk to cover me. Liz darts out of the cabin and fills two pans full of snow before returning to get more containers. I hear Liz and Enuk behind me as I head out into the open.

I'm trying to watch for the Wendigo but have to focus on getting the limbs back to the cabin as fast as I can. The first one I try is almost too large for me to drag. I get it back and Enuk has to help me get it in the door. We'll cut it up later in the relative safety of the cabin.

Liz fills up everything she can find with snow. I make three trips with good sized limbs. On my fourth trip, I smell the musky odor of death and corruption over by the stand of trees. I grab a smaller limb and haul ass back to the cabin. "It's here," I yell as I run for my life.

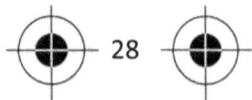

I see Enuk bring up his rifle and fire at something over my right shoulder. "BANG...BANG" I dare not look and just run as fast as I can into the cabin, dragging the branch with me. Once inside I drop the limb and move to the door. Enuk knocks me out of the way, as he leaps through the door and swings the door shut. He pushes himself up against the door, trying to get the bolt closed when the Wendigo slams into the door knocking him back. I am lying prone in front of the door with the Wendigo standing above me in the doorway. It lets out its deafening howl and I know I'm going to die.

I'm so startled by how much it looks like an emaciated Caleb I manage to speak. "Caleb...Caleb, it's me, Logan," I stammer.

The Wendigo glares at me and I see recognition flash in it's eyes. It stops it's advance and just stares back at me. In that instant it's black dead eyes become the human eyes of Caleb. Enuk uses the distraction to slam the door right into the Wendigo, knocking it out of the threshold. Enuk throws the bolt on the door and starts shoving anything he can find in front of the door.

I just sit there on the floor, thinking about what just happened. The Wendigo recognized me, I know it did. Is it possible that the Caleb I knew is still inside that thing somewhere? I wonder if I could somehow change him back.

After several minutes we feel secure enough to start cutting up the wood and melting the snow. Liz is rattled but doing ok. I ask her to start melting the snow and I think she is just thankful to be doing something helpful.

The eerie howl of the Wendigo comes from outside. All of us tense and grab weapons. Even Liz has her hand on a pot of boiling water ready to throw it at whatever might crash through our door. I'm thankful we are all dealing with our fear better. We will need to channel that fear into positive action if we are going to survive.

We work in silence just getting what needs to be done finished. Then Liz brings up what has been on all our minds. "Um…I really have to go to the bathroom," she admits, starting to squirm a little.

"I've been thinking about that and I sure don't want to squat down outside with that thing out there. I think the best thing is to use a corner of the other room. I do have this," I offer, holding out a roll of toilet paper.

I can tell this whole situation is unacceptable to Liz but she is starting to dance from having to pee so badly. She grabs the toilet paper and goes into the other room. When she opens the door, she takes a step back from the stench of death that washes over her. We threw all the human remains we found in the cabin into that room.

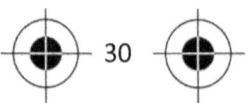

Liz comes out a short time later and puts the roll of toilet paper on the floor next to the door. Enuk and I take turns venturing into the bathroom of death.

Liz has a deck of cards so the three of us play blackjack and poker to pass the time. We joke around and even start to enjoy getting to know each other. About the time we relax and forget there is a human flesh-craving beast just outside our door, we hear it's wailing howl. All of us stiffen and get ready to fight. There is silence for a couple of intense minutes, then the smallest of scratches on the door. Over and over, the scratches come from the door. It sounds like an animal is running its claws lightly over the lower corner of the door. I wonder if it's taunting us. As if we are playthings to it.

The scratching is taking it's toll on my companions. They are both about ready to lose it. "Stop it!" Liz screams as she runs over to the door and pounds on it.

Something bashes the door from the outside almost breaking the wooden bolt. Enuk and I heave ourselves against the door to brace it as the Wendigo flings itself into the door repeatedly. This new situation brings Liz back to her senses and she stands back, ready to hit the beast with the red-hot poker from the fire. After about five bashes into the door, it stops and everything goes quiet.

We stay alert for a while but eventually settle back down to having some food and playing cards. The normalcy of doing familiar things keeps us sane.

We go to sleep as early as we can stand it because we don't know what the night will bring. Liz beds down right next to me and snuggles up tight. She falls asleep and I soon follow her into dreamland.

In my dream, I'm in a club with Liz, dirty dancing. The pounding of the beat of the music is pumping through me. The feel of Liz's body next to mine is making me so hot. I'm sweating and the air is so full of smoke. I start to cough and believe this is a dream. I cough more and more as the club fills with smoke.

I wake up choking. The cabin is full of smoke. Something has blocked up the chimney. Is the Wendigo that smart? I shake Liz awake and yell at Enuk. "Get up! Enuk! The cabin is filling with smoke. It must be the Wendigo. Get ready to fight!" I warn as I'm pulling on my boots.

I grab my knife in one hand and a torch in the other. Enuk gets his knife, gun and a torch. Liz grabs the red-hot poker and we all go out the door into the cold darkness of the night. The night is very still and freezing cold. No animal noises, not even the sound of the wind breaks the unnatural silence. Even though we can't see it, we can smell the Wendigo's retched stench of death all around. Enuk and I swing our torches, trying to catch a glimpse of the deadly creature.

All of the sudden, the Wendigo is just there. It savagely attacks Enuk, who falls back onto the ground, blood splattering everywhere.

I yell "Caleb!" As the beast turns to look at me, I stick my torch into its face and slice its chest open with my red-hot knife tip.

"WaaaEee!" It screams in pain and staggers back. I press my attack, poking it with the torch again and again, driving it away. It turns and runs into the darkness.

I go back to Liz and Enuk. Enuk is getting to his feet. He has been deeply clawed down his right shoulder, making his arm useless. I move us so the wall of the cabin is at our back.

"You two stay here. I'll try to clear the flue so we can go back inside the cabin. Liz, you take the other torch," I command, taking a moment to smile at Liz. She grabs me and gives me a good passionate kiss for luck.

I head around the cabin and up the snow to the roof. I've my knife and rifle. It's slow going but I make it onto the roof. Clumps of tall grass have been shoved into the chimney. I start digging it out with my knife. As I'm about done digging out the grass, I hear Liz scream. "Ahhh…"

I look over the edge of the roof and see the Wendigo attacking Enuk and Liz. They are both wildly swinging torches at it. The Wendigo slashes into Enuk, splattering blood upon the white snow. I know I do not have time to get around to them in time, so without thinking I jump onto the Wendigo's back knife in hand. I crash down upon the Wendigo driving my knife to the hilt between the beast's shoulder blades.

"WaaaEee!" the Wendigo screams and tries to buck me off its back. The jump and the thrashing of the Wendigo knocks me off, leaving my knife embedded in its back as it runs off into the darkness.

"Liz go back in the cabin," I order, as I try to get Enuk to his feet but it's just no good.

Enuk's gut has been sliced open and I can see his intestines. He is using both hands to keep his guts in his body. We both know that unless he gets help immediately he is going to die. I pick him up and carry him inside, then go back out and get his gun and torch.

As I look Enuk over, Liz bolts and blockades the door. The cabin is still smoky but it seems more important to be inside behind the bolted door right now.

"Liz get me some shirts out of Enuk's pack and a belt if you can find one," I order, knowing no matter what I do, Enuk will probably die.

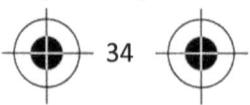

Liz gets me the stuff and I pack his wound with the shirts and put the belt around him. Enuk winces with pain several times, as I pull the belt tight but never cries out. He is a strong warrior and my friend. I hate to see him die like this. I cover his shoulder to try and stop the bleeding but it's no good.

I search Enuk's face and he nods to me. We both know he is going to die. Nothing has to be said between us. We have both seen enough death to understand it. I help Enuk lie back and we all sit in silence.

Liz is standing way back, watching us. I can see the turmoil building inside her and know she will soon have to break the silence. The Wendigo howls off in the distance reminding us that this is not over.

"Is he going to die?" Liz just blurts out, not able to contain herself any longer.

When I don't immediately answer, Enuk speaks. "Use my body to lure the beast away from you when the time comes. It craves human flesh. The time it takes to feast on my body may be enough for you to get to the chopper." Enuk mutters, grasping for my hand. I put my hand in his and he squeezes tight trying to hold back the pain.

I nod my head and Liz turns ash white. She understands right then that Enuk is dying. Liz turns away and starts to cry bringing her arms over her stomach, as though she were suddenly very cold.

Enuk motions for me to come closer. "Do what you can to send my spirit to my ancestors," Enuk whispers to me.

"I will perform the rites I know," I promise, nodding my head.

"I will not need my knife where I am going and I would be honored if you would carry it my friend." Enuk pushes his knife into my hand.

"You live to tell this tale, Logan. Do not let revenge overshadow your heart. You live to tell my people what happened here," Enuk orders, squeezing my hand with all the strength he has left.

I sit with him as he slowly slips away. Enuk occasionally smoked so I look in his pack for his tobacco and pipe. I light the pipe and perform every rite I can even remember hearing over Enuk. I know he is near death and I aim to keep my promise. Enuk and I both know that having one's body devoured by a cursed beast like a Wendigo will most likely damn his spirit. In offering us the use of his body to distract the Wendigo, Enuk is probably sacrificing his soul.

As Enuk's last breath leaves him, I get up and dance for his spirit. I blow the tobacco smoke over his body and to the four directions. I do everything I can think of to help his spirit be at rest. I know Liz is watching me and must think I've lost it, but I don't care. I'm doing what I can for my friend, Enuk.

When I have done all I can for his soul, I pull his body into a cleared area of the other room and put his blanket over him. I wash his blood off my hands as best I can and go lie over next to Liz.

Liz rolls over to look at me. She has a crazed look in her eyes. I wonder if this has all been too much for her. She starts kissing me and then I know what she wants. She wants to lose herself in orgasm so she can sleep. I'm too tired to argue with her and know it will help her. I figure the best thing is to just get it over with. I move my hand down to her pants to work on her button. But instead, she pushes me on my back and climbs on top. She pulls off her shirt revealing her milky white breasts. She pulls my shirt off and I realize that she wants to really go at it.

She feeds me her perfect breasts and moans in ecstasy as I take them into my mouth. We are like animals in a mating frenzy. We tear at each other's remaining clothes and are soon naked. We join together again and again until we finally fall upon our bedding totally spent. I pull the blankets over us and let sleep take me.

Chapter 3: Escape

I awake in a naked tangle with Liz. I know it's still dark outside but the fire is going out. I get up and put some more wood on the fire. Looking at Liz naked under the covers, all I want is to just crawl back beside her, but I know the best thing is to get dressed in case we have an unwanted visitor and I need to act fast. I pull on my cold clothes and then snuggle up to Liz. She mutters a little from the feel of chill beside her naked body but soon settles into her sleeping rhythm again. I listen to Liz's muffled breathing. It calms me and soon I'm able to fall back to sleep.

I wake up and move around the cabin a little before Liz wakes up. The sun is up and I just can't sleep anymore. Liz looks at me and the realization of what happened between us flushes her cheeks. She looks at her naked body and turns away from me. I feel ashamed and don't really know why. She wanted everything we did, I know she did. I guess this situation is too much for her. She reaches out and gets her clothes. Then under the covers, she gets dressed. I don't like the awkward silence so I decide to break it.

"Liz, you want something to eat?"

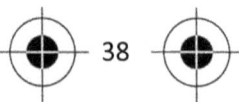

"Um…sure," she replies, still not looking at me.

I bring some biscuits and jam to her. She half smiles at me and takes the plate. I sit next to her and share the biscuits with her. She soon warms up and I feel things are good between us. We play cards until around noon. Then we hear the distant howl of the Wendigo and Liz gets scared. I hold up my arm and Liz snuggles under it. She holds on to me for some time before releasing her grip. She looks in my eyes with her large blue eyes and I can tell she is counting on me to save her. I smile at her. "It will be all right, Liz. We'll be out of here by this time tomorrow."

"God I hope so," she whispers in my ear.

I nibble on her ear. She returns my interest. Soon she is in a sexual frenzy. Again our clothes go flying. She is totally into our lovemaking. It's savage and animalistic. We go for as long as we can and then start again. I know she wants to wear herself out so she can slip back into her safe dreams. It's wonderful animal sex. Finally she is sated and crumples into a heap on the covers. I cover us and sleep next to her.

I wake to violent pounding on the door. I rush to the door butt naked trying to reinforce it. Liz comes to my side and we both push on the door, naked as the day we were born. A board next to Liz's head splinters and cuts into her a little. She moves back behind me as the Wendigo waves its hand violently through the opening. It's trying to claw us as it wildly flails its hand around. "Get the poker!" I yell to Liz.

Liz runs to the fire and comes back with the red-hot poker. She tries to give it to me but I have to hold the door shut. "Stab it!" I order.

Liz jabs the hot poker into the Wendigo's arm and it lets out a howl of pain. "WaaaEee!" It screams as it withdraws its arm.

It pounds on the door a couple more times and then all is silent. Liz is standing nude next to me still holding the hot poker breathing hard. She is quite a sight all naked and taking charge with her weapon. Right then, I realize I really like Liz. "Damn you look hot!"

She looks at me and smiles. That smile lets me know she feels the same about me. I reinforce the door and get some wood to cover the hole in the door. "Go lie down, Liz. I'll be done in a minute."

Liz puts the poker back into the fire and crawls under the covers. She watches me as I work and I can tell that as long as that damn Wendigo doesn't disturb us again we are going to have some more wild sex. A few minutes later, I find out that I was right. We have crazy animal sex and fall back to sleep.

The next morning comes and I know the chopper should be here around 9am. They will be expecting to meet us at the drop off point but will fly over the

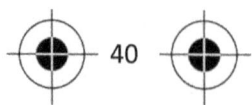

cabin if we are not there. I intend to wait for them right here.

This morning Liz is very friendly and we have some short morning sex. It's unlike any of the other times. It is tender and loving. I can tell Liz has become emotionally attached to me. I know she is my woman now. I don't know how long it will last back in the real world but here and now, she is all mine and I'm all hers.

I make six torches to put around us when we go outside. I get a fire bundle that I can throw on the ground and easily light as a signal fire and help to keep the Wendigo at bay.

I hate to do it but I drag Enuk's body out of the backroom. Liz looks at me and I know she hates it too. It might just give us the edge we need.

Right after 9am, I hear the chopper. I roll Enuk's body out the door, and then Liz and I head out of the cabin. I place the torches in a circle and light the fire bundle. Liz has the red-hot poker in her hand. I've Enuk's knife in my right hand and a torch in the other. I drag Enuk's body outside the ring of torches. The chopper comes into view above us and old Buck waves to us. I point at Enuk's lifeless body and motion for him to drop a rope. He nods and soon a rope is dangling before us. The noise and wind from the helicopter makes it almost impossible to watch for the Wendigo.

I tie the rope on Liz and kiss her. I motion for Buck to start pulling her up. Her feet leave the ground right as I see the Wendigo rush at us. I brace for its attack but it leaps into the air upon Liz. She is just out of my reach and the Wendigo is upon her. "Help me Logan...HELP ME PLEASE...AHHH!" Liz desperately screams.

The Wendigo's claws dig into Liz's beautiful flesh. Blood splatters me and Buck has a hard time getting the chopper under control with the extra weight on the rope. I try to jump into the air to reach Liz but it's no use. The wench is still slowly taking her and the Wendigo up to the chopper. More blood washes over me as the Wendigo bites into Liz's neck and swallows the chunk of flesh. Liz looks at me and her eyes are begging me to help her. I pull out my rife and shoot the Wendigo. It looks at me and bears its teeth. I see hate in its black eyes.

Buck stops the wench and Liz and the Wendigo swing in the air just below the helicopter. The Wendigo looks up and it's close enough to get into the chopper. It climbs in and Buck swerves the chopper away from the cabin. It flies off with Liz's lifeless body hanging below it like some unholy piñata.

The chopper goes over a ridge and then there is an awful thunderous sound as the helicopter crashes, exploding into a ball of fire. I hope that is the end of the Wendigo but I fear it still lives. I quickly rush

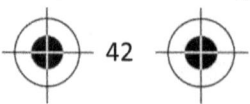

inside the cabin and grab everything I might need. I throw another fire bundle into the cabin upon the woodpile. I grab Enuk's body and throw it on the fire. I hope this will help send his spirit to his ancestors. It has to be better than letting the Wendigo devour his flesh. I pull his medicine bag off him to keep for his family. Most people will not believe the truth about what happened here. I feel it's better to get rid of evidence that I don't want to try to explain. I say a few words over the dead, grab my pack and weapons before heading out towards the only civilization I know at Goose Creek about fifty miles away to the south.

Thankfully, the chopper went down in the opposite direction from where I'm heading. I have walked a couple miles when I hear an eerier howl that could be the wind or the Wendigo far away. I just keep going, because that is all I can do. I walk even into the night until I can go no further. I sleep sitting propped up next to a tree with Enuk's knife in my hand.

After a couple hours of sleep, I'm too cold to sleep anymore so I get to my feet and slowly keep going. Thankfully there is almost a full moon so I can see my way. I move slowly because I know a fall could hurt me bad enough to make this trip impossible. I trudge on until dawn comes.

In the first rays of the morning sun, I stop for a rest and a snack. I chew on a biscuit and remember sharing them with Liz, all naked and comfortable. Her smile haunts me as it turns into her begging eyes, pleading with me to save her. I physically shake my head to get the image out of my head. I get back up and start waking. Back home when I was younger I could run over fifty miles in a day. I can do this, I keep telling myself.

Around midday, I take a break and have a couple of slices of cheese. I scan the horizon and know I'm within striking distance of Goose Creek. The weather has turned warmer, which is good and bad. It makes traveling over the snow much more slick but it's good to not be so cold. I have to really concentrate to keep myself from sweating. If I get wet from sweat, I could freeze to death or at least catch a chill I can not shake. I still have too far to go to mess up now. Suddenly I get a whiff of a musky smell of corruption and death. I know the Wendigo is up wind of me and close. I take out my knife and move into a stand of trees. I crouch down, get my rifle ready and watch. I become the hunter I've grown up training to be. I'm as a rock, unmoving and silent.

Soon the gaunt figure of Caleb strides into view. It goes right to the log I was just sitting on and sniffs the air looking around. I center my shot on his head,

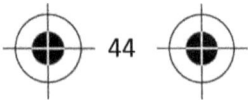

let out my breath and squeeze the trigger. "BANG!" my rifle reports.

The Wendigo looks right at me as the bullet slices into the side of its neck. "WaaaEee!" It screams as it launches itself towards me. I fire again and again before it's on me. "BANG...BANG" the rifle thunders. The beast staggers a little when my last shot hits it square over where its heart should be.

I drop the rifle and meet the Wendigo's charge with Enuk's knife. It leaps on me catching my left shoulder with its claws. I slice my knife across its chest as we tumble to the ground. I slash at it as savagely as it claws at me. We are more animals than men fighting to the death. We both scream our death cries as we take the blood of the other. I chop at its head and partially scalp it. I manage to stab it in the left side between its ribs up into where the heart should be. It screams worse than I've ever heard anything scream. "WaaaEeeAaaWaaaEee!"

It pulls itself free from my knife and limps off. I consider following it but I'm badly hurt and there is still some fight left in it. I manage to get to my feet, feeling my shoulders agony increase as I move. The claw marks burn like fire and I am temporarily overcome by the intense pain. Stalled I consider just lying down in the snow. I know I have to move now or I may never again. I'm not really sure why, but I take the scalp of hair I cut off the beast. I then force myself to put one foot in front of the other. It is a test of will. My body is all in and I'm pushing it beyond its limits. I know I'm losing blood and am close to passing out. I just concentrate on that next step. It's all about that next step.

It's night before I see the lights of Goose Creek. I walk as far as I can before falling into the snow. I then fire my rifle repeatedly until I'm out of ammunition. I hear voices as I slip into the welcoming darkness.

Chapter 4:
Old Broken Nose

I am in a forest wandering. I'm dressed in the traditional dress of my ancient ancestors. I am me but yet not me. I am here but yet not here. I am like a spirit that can sense the world but is invisible to it. I can walk, smell, hear and see but cannot touch anything.

I walk out of a forest and see two great men talking. One is taller and of a noble bearing. He is wearing the finest buckskins and is surely a chief among chiefs. The other man is dressed in worn rags and leans on a staff, like a grandfather. He seems to be an ancient being and carries a turtle shell rattle on his belt. The two men are talking.

"I made this land and soon I will populate it with men," the Chief insists.

"No, I made this land," Grandfather argues, moving his arm to encompass all he sees.

"Let us test our skill and then you will know I created this land," the Chief suggests.

"I can move that mountain over there," Grandfather claims.

"Fine, whoever can move that mountain farther can claim to have made this land," the Chief agrees.

"I will go first. But first you must turn your back so you cannot see and then steal my magic," Grandfather insists.

The great Chief looks offended at the suggestion that he would steal the old man's magic but turns around anyway. There is a mighty rumbling and Grandfather speaks. "You may turn around and see how I have moved the mountain," Grandfather gloats proudly.

The Chief turns around and sees that the mountain has indeed been moved but only a small distance. He looks surprised and turns his wary eyes upon grandfather. "You do have strong magic but now it is my turn. Turn your back and I shall move the mountain further than you," the Chief vows.

Grandfather turns his back and a mighty rumbling occurs. The ground shakes and Grandfather leans heavy on his stick to not fall. As the rumbling starts to subside Grandfather cannot wait any longer and he suddenly turns around to see what has been done to the mountain. However, the chief has moved the mountain right behind Grandfather and he smashes his face into the mountain breaking his nose to one side.

"Ahh…I should have waited for you to tell me you were done," Grandfather Broken Nose admits.

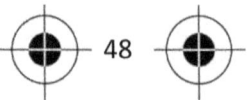 48

"I am not sure what to do with you. I cannot have you roaming the land with your powerful magic. What if you hurt the men I am going to make?" the Chief considers.

"I can help these men. I can move the winds up and over their lands. I can also drive the spirits of disease and sickness away from them. I can also give them power over beasts of magic," Grandfather Broken Nose, says looking right at me.

"How will the people call upon you when they need your help?" the Chief asks.

"I will come to a few of the men who have the gift to see beyond what is before them. I will come to them in their dreams. These few men will go into the forest until a tree calls to them. In that tree, they will carve a mask to honor me. In so doing, a small piece of my spirit will inhabit the mask and be able to call to me when the men wear it. Then I will come to protect the people from harsh winds and sickness," Grandfather Broken Nose vows.

"This is good. If you do this, you can live in the deep forests and underground caves I have made," the Chief offers.

Grandfather Broken Nose turns and looks right at me. "You, Logan, need to take up your friend's knife and carve a mask of the beast. Use its own hair and the blood you share to make the mask. Pay the mask for its service and you will gain power over that which hunts you. Go, Logan, become what you must to protect the people," Grandfather Broken Nose commands as a bright light blinds me.

I wake up in a hospital bed with bright light shining in my face. The pretty blond nurse tells me I was found just outside Goose Creek six days ago. I was badly mauled by a bear and they feared I wasn't going to make it.

Officially did die right after I arrived at the hospital for almost eight minutes. For the rest of my life, I will carry a nasty scar of the Wendigo on my left shoulder but should fully recover.

I go with the bear story the police have pieced together. It seems much easier than trying to explain a Wendigo.

Before I leave to head home, I seek out Enuk's father and tell him the true tale of Bear Ridge. He listens to every word and at the end, I give him Enuk's medicine pouch and knife. He thanks me and wishes me safe journey. He gives me Enuk's knife back, telling me I still have need of it. I feel honored that I got the chance to tell his father that Enuk died a warrior and that he saved my life.

Chapter 5:
Agent Johansson

The night before I'm scheduled to fly back to college, there is a knock at the door of my apartment.

When I open the door, I'm surprised to see a good-looking woman in a business suit. It's kind of hard to guess her age but I would say around thirty. She has dark hair that is put up in a perfect bun. Her manner of dress, hair and makeup all scream of meticulous perfection. She is wearing designer sunglasses even though it is nighttime. She definitely has a presence of authority. I bet if she were wearing something where you could really see her figure and let her hair down, she would be a real head turner.

"Mr. Logan Longstride?" she inquires, looking at my comfortable clothes and beyond to my messy room.

"Yes," I say, still admiring her figure.

"I am Agent Johansson with the FBI, may I come in?" she asks, I can tell she is examining every detail.

"Um…sure," I stammer, standing aside to let her in.

She goes over to a chair next to a small table and pushes a couple of my textbooks out of the way so she can sit down. She looks expectantly at me and I hurry over to sit across from her. She is definitely used to being in charge.

"I want to inquire about the recent events up at Bear Ridge," Agent Johansson announces, taking out a file out of her slim bag and placing it on the table precisely in front of her.

Before I can respond, she starts asking questions in a matter the fact way. "You said in your statement that your rescue group found no survivors. Is that correct?" Agent Johansson probes, looking up at me. I feel like she will see right through any lies I might try to tell her.

"Yes," I agree, looking away from her watchful eyes.

"How did the members of your rescue party die?" Agent Johansson asks, making notes on her paperwork.

"I was told, it was believed to be a bear attack," I offer, still sticking to my story.

Agent Johansson takes off her sunglasses, carefully folds them and lays then on the table just so. She then stares at me with sharp green eyes that I can tell have seen way too much to take any shit from the likes of me. "I didn't ask what the report says. I asked how the four members of the ground rescue team and your bush pilot actually died," Agent Johansson demands, staring into me.

I'm taken aback by how forceful and direct she is. "What do you want me to say?" I ask.

"I want the truth. No one with any real sense would buy a story where four people were mauled to death by a bear. Especially when two members of the group were armed with rifles that could easily bring down a bear and are both very skilled hunters." Agent Johansson leans toward me. It feels like she is trying to crowd the truth out of me. "It is also too convenient that the only physical evidence was destroyed when the cabin and chopper both burned. So what really happened?" Agent Johansson presses me, glaring.

"I think I'm probably better off sticking to the bear story," I insist, leaning back in my chair. I want to put some space between me and Agent Johansson to try to regain some control of the conversation.

"That may be good enough for the locals but it won't fly with me. My agency needs the truth," Agent Johansson demands.

"You would lock me up in a loony bin if I told you the truth."

Agent Johansson relaxes a little. "Can I have a glass of water?"

I get her a glass of water. She is definitely less aggressive right now and her manner puts me at ease.

I bet she can snap back into interrogation mode in a moment but her current demeanor does not even suggest that.

"Ok, let's start again. It is just you and me and I'm not recording this. Anything you say to me you can deny later. I just want to know the truth about what happened on Bear Ridge," She offers, putting down her pen at an exact angle to the file lying before her.

I figure what the hell. I'll tell her part of it and see how she reacts. "When we got to the cabin we found evidence that one of the members of the lost group had cannibalized the others."

Agent Johansson is not startled at all and just nods. This worries me but I continue.

I get up and walk to the near window, not wanting to look at Agent Johansson in the face. "We were then attacked by a naked man that was more beast than man. He is the one that killed everyone," I say, not wanting to tell her who the Wendigo used to be. I turn to look how she reacts.

She looks up at me not really surprised, but as if she is studying me. "What is a cannibal of men called by the Seneca?" Agent Johansson probes, but I think she already knows. I think she already knew everything I told her but I've no idea how.

"Wendigo," I almost spit out the word. I have a lot of anger towards Caleb and what he has become. I

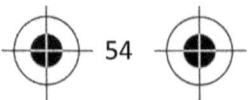

hope he died out there in the snow, but I bet he is still out there looking for his next victim.

"You are quite a man to have survived such an encounter." Agent Johansson admits, taking a couple moments to really look me over again to see if she missed anything.

"How do you know so much about what happened at Bear Ridge?" I ask, taking a couple steps toward her.

"It is my job to know. The official record will stand with the bear attack story," Agent Johansson says as she gets up and looks to be leaving, gathering her papers and stacking them neatly in her folder.

"That's it? I tell you we found a man who became a cannibal so he turned into a flesh-eating monster called a Wendigo and that's it. It's probably out there right now killing and eating people," I warn, walking up and taking her arm to turn her toward me.

"What can be done, will be done. You are a civilian and are no longer part of the situation. I recommend you go back to college and forget this ever happened," Agent Johansson suggests, pulling away from me and putting her sunglasses back on.

"Never happened? Are you crazy or something? My cousin Caleb was the one that turned into that monster. I will never forget the recognition in it's dead eyes when it saw me. Some part of my friend, my blood brother, is locked forever in torment inside that beast. I will find a way to kill it and come back to set the spirit of Caleb free," I vow, getting all worked up.

Agent Johansson almost smiles at me. "Join us. My organization will give you the resources you need," Agent Johansson says, with an intense look even through her sunglasses.

Her statement shocks me back to my senses. Something is going on that I do not fully understand. I bet Agent Johansson doesn't even work for the FBI. She knows way too much about things that most people write off as superstition and myth. I don't relish being at such a huge disadvantage. When I go after game, I like to have the upper hand. It seems to me that Agent Johansson is the hunter and I've just walked into her trap. I bet she wanted me to join her "organization" from the moment she walked in my door. She set the bait and I went right for it. Damn she's good.

"What organization do you belong to?" I ask, wondering if I will even get a straight answer.

"The FBI among others. Let's just say that as a member of my organization you would have access to information, manpower, resources and tools to make a difference in the world. We could help you deal with the Wendigo as well."

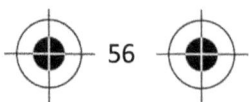

"So you want me to join some secret monster hunting organization?" I joke.

"Something like that, yes," Agent Johansson does smile then, a faint smile that makes her look younger.

What do I have myself into? I had no idea there was such an organization. I do intend to come back and hunt the Wendigo after I straighten my life out a bit and make the mask of the Wendigo to gain power over it. I know it was just a dream but it was so real to me. I will carve the mask of the Wendigo and gain power over it. No matter what else happens, I know that will come to pass.

"I will not deny that I'm intrigued by your offer. I have some personal business to attend to, but after that, I will be hunting the Wendigo. If your group wants to help with that, then I would accept it."

Agent Johansson pulls a cell phone out of her bag and hands it to me. My number is on the phone. Call me when you are ready. Have fun at college," Agent Johansson turns and heads to the door.

"Yeah, oh joy. College is going to suck. I've missed seven weeks and finals are next week. I will probably have to take the whole damn semester over," I mutter, more to myself than to her.

"Oh I wouldn't worry yourself about it too much…Take care Logan. Don't let the Wendigo bite," Agent Johansson teases me as she walks out my door and closes it behind her.

I look at the cell in my hand and think, damn that was weird. I wonder if I will ever have the nerve to call Agent Johansson. She is one cool chick. If she is any example of her organization, I bet they really could help me with the Wendigo.

Chapter 6: Heritage

I return to college to try to salvage my semester even though finals are next week. I go to my professor's one after the other and they are all way to understanding. They give me copies of the notes I missed and offer me advice for the final. It's weird they all have these same blue folders with sample tests and notes all neatly laid out. The chance of them all preparing the same color folders labeled out exactly the same with dividers and everything is impossible. Agent Johansson must have made this happen. I guess she wants me to get my personal life in order as fast as possible.

I dedicate myself to studying the blue folders and try to forget about Caleb and Bear Ridge. I take my finals and get the grades I need to graduate college with an Anthropology degree and a minor in History.

My family would have come for graduation but I didn't even tell them I am back yet. I don't have time to wait around for the ceremony anyway. Caleb and I should be walking that stage together getting the pieces of paper that we worked so hard for. The whole thing just seems so hollow without him.

On the journey home, I take some time to remember Caleb and my youth. I was born Logan Fletcher Longstride on the Allegany Indian Reservation, located in the southwest corner of New York State. I am a full-blooded Seneca which also makes me part of the Iroquois Confederacy. Around four hundred years ago the Cayugas, Mohowks, Senecas, Oneidas and Onondaga joined together to form the Iroquois Confederacy. They planted the Tree of Peace and lived together as one nation. Later, the Tuscaroras also joined the Iroquois Confederacy. This is my great heritage even though many have forgotten it. We who once roamed huge areas of land are herded onto small tracks of unwanted land and left to rot. Many members of our tribe are still stagnant but some have managed to grow strong in adversity. Many of the young who manage to get away from the reservation never look back. I was raised better and will always honor my past.

My mother is Sally Longstride and Orrin Longstride is my father. They raised me with lots of help from both sets of grandparents. We have lived on the reservation all my life. My father used to work at the local dam that was built in the sixties. When the dam was built, it flooded over 10,000 acres of our tribal land, taking a third of our land from us. My mother worked as a schoolteacher on the reservation.

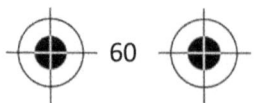

All Seneca have a clan they belong to. Clans are groups of families that share a common female ancestry and are named after animals that assist the Seneca. My clan is that of the Hawk. Seneca lineage, including clan and tribe, descends from the mother.

When I was sixteen, my father was in a car wreck that left him in a wheelchair. This really affected my mother. My father had always been the strong man she could lean on. She tried to stay around and nurse my father back to health but it tore at her every day. She ended up losing her teaching job because she had to care for my father. She took a job at the reservation casino right after I left for college and lost herself to that world. She took other lovers and would not come home for weeks at a time. When she did come home, she was usually drunk and only stayed a couple days before disappearing again. My grandparents and father did what they could for my mother but she was just too lost. My parents are still married but my mom has not lived at home for four years.

My grandma on my father's side, Hope Longstride is a renowned storyteller, author and a leader of our tribe. She would tell me all the stories of the Seneca and Iroquois. She helped me understand how to live in the present but remember the past.

Grandma Longstride is the Clan Mother of our reservation. Within the Seneca tribe, women have historically been held with high regard, possessing power and responsibility to their clan and tribe. Traditionally the oldest woman of a clan is known as the Clan Mother. The Clan Mother has the responsibility for naming all members of their clans. In the past Clan Mothers had the right to command a war party to avenge the death of a loved one or to find a likely candidate to adopt.

My other grandmother, Judith Seneca is a good simple woman who still lives day to day by the old ways. She showed me much of how to live without the modern conveniences that so many of us have come to depend on. By the time I was a teenager, I thought she was kind of crazy for living that way, but now that I'm a little bit wiser, I understand her better. She is one of the last of my people who really applies the old ways of living to daily life. When all the people like her are gone, how will the young ever truly understand their heritage? Sure, they can read about it in a book, but that is nothing compared to actually sharing in the experience as grandmother Seneca has often done with me.

From the time I could walk, I was going with my family to everything. My father would take me hunting all the time. We often just wandered the forest not really wanting to kill anything. However, when the opportunity arose my father was a great hunter and many a day we came home with dinner. During the summer, I would often travel up north into Canada and Alaska with my grandparents as they went to counsel meeting or great hunting trips. In this way, I learned the old ways of hunting.

My cousin Caleb Keeshig was my age and we often traveled together with our shared grandparents. Caleb was like a brother to me. When we were twelve, we even became blood brothers. We sliced open our thumbs and let our blood run together. We grew up together and went to college together. I cannot believe he is gone now, trapped inside that infernal Wendigo.

Caleb and I used to spend a lot of our time playing lacrosse. Lacrosse was played by the Iroquois long before the white man set foot on North America. Caleb and I got so good at lacrosse that we got scholarships to college. Those scholarships let us go out into the world and have opportunities we would have never had. It is funny how a game with a ball and hooped sticks can affect so much.

My father and both my grandfathers, Jubal Seneca and Amos Longstride, are members of the False Face Society. I'm not supposed to know they are members but living so close to them for so long, I figured it out. The False Face Society is a group of men who have been given a dream from Old Broken Nose, who is also known as False Face. Once a dream is received, the person goes into the woods until a basswood tree calls to him. The masks are carved directly on the living tree. When the mask is complete, it is cut from the tree. The crafter takes the mask to a secluded area and works on it until it is done. The mask will be polished, painted and hair, feathers and other things the owner feels are necessary are added. Masks are painted black if they were begun in the afternoon and red if they were begun in the morning. Red masks are considered more powerful as are morning rituals.

Masks carved into trees that are alive, are considered to be living and breathing beings. Their maker serves them white corn mush and small pouches of tobacco tied in their hair as payment for their help.

The members of the False Face use the masks to invoke Old Broken Nose when the people need help. Old Broken Nose has the power to redirect the winds up and over the people's land. He also has the power to drive off spirits that bring sickness and disease.

Twice a year, the False Face Society gather to tell the story of Old Broken Nose, invoke the spirits using tobacco, perform the main False Face ritual, and pass out corn mush at the closing.

The False Face members, wearing their masks go through all houses in the community, driving away evil spirits, disease and sickness. They open every window and door. They put out any hearth fires and rekindle new ones. The False Face members shake turtle shell rattles and rub them along the walls and

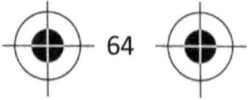

floors of the homes. Any sick people found are cleansed by performing a healing rite involving tobacco and singing. The tobacco is burned and smoked to invoke Old Broken Nose and wood ashes from the house's hearth are blown over the ill person.

The community gathers at the main meetinghouse, often called a longhouse. The people bring tobacco to the members of the False Face who sit on the floor and burn it. This renews and strengthens the bond of the village and the False Face Society. It also strengthens the power of the False Face masks and their connection to Old Broken Nose. The ceremony continues with a dance. At the closing of the ritual, corn mush is passed out to the community and everyone returns to their cleansed homes.

The ceremony is performed during the fall and spring as well as during the Midwinter Festival. Occasionally a member of the community will ask the False Face Society to cleanse a sickness or home as needed throughout the year.

I have a vivid memory of the power a mask of Grandfather Broken Nose can give. When I was sixteen, I heard a horrible sound of crushing and scraping metal. I ran outside and saw my father's car crumpled into a truck. I ran to the car and tried to pull my father free. There was gasoline on the ground and my father was trapped behind the steering wheel. Lying next to my father was his black mask. He had just come from the house of a friend who was sick. I didn't know what to do so I grabbed the mask and put it on my father. Almost at once, his breathing became more regular and he calmed down. Then in this calm almost otherworldly voice, he spoke to me in our native tongue. "Logan, calm yourself. Your father will survive, but you must help him. Reach down and move his seat back."

I looked at my father and saw his eyes were closed. I didn't know what was going on but I did as I was told. I moved back his seat and he slumped over toward me. I caught him in my arms.

"You must drag your father away from the car. The fire spirits are angry and will soon show their fury." Says the same strange voice from where my father's unmoving lips are.

I drag my father far away from the car. He was totally dead weight and it was hard for me to move him. I lost my grip several times and fall upon the road. But each time I got up and pulled that much harder. When I have pulled all I could, both of the cars erupt in fire. I know I saved my father's life. Only then do I wonder about the people in the other car.

As if in an answer to my very thoughts a voice comes from beneath the mask. "You could not have saved them. The Great Spirit had already taken them away. Now quickly hide me so that no one will steal my magic."

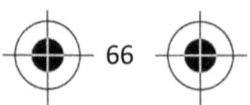

I run to the house and hide my father's mask in my room. I'm back by my father's side by the time the police arrive.

I've thought about that evening many times and tried to bring it up with my father. But he never spoke of it and I never had the courage to. I rationalized it away with my belief that my father was just playing his part as a member of the False Face Society. But now I think maybe Grandfather Broken Nose spoke to me directly though my father's mask.

These are the beliefs I was taught. When I was younger, I believed all of the stories and rituals. As I grew older, I lost some of my unquestioning faith but I never forgot. Now I know that at least some of the stories are true and my faith is renewed. I'm returning home to make my own mask and join the ranks of the False Face Society.

Chapter 7:
Home

I arrive at my dad's house around dinnertime on Thursday night. He is expecting me and greets me at the door. Tonight it's just the two of us. I know tomorrow I will have to see the whole family and I'm looking forward to it. I've not been home since Christmas, almost six months ago and I missed them.

"Howdy son, you're looking well," Dad exclaims, looking me over.

"It's good to be home. It has been a long couple of months," I confess, bending down to hug my dad. I can smell the wood smoke in his hair, a comforting odor.

"Yeah that was a hell of a thing about Caleb getting killed by a bear. I still can't believe it. He was as good a hunter as you or I, and I've just never heard of a bear going after so many people at once," Dad admits as he scratches his chin.

"I will tell the story tomorrow for you and my grandfathers. Tonight let's just enjoy being a family. Hey, where's Faith?" I ask, noticing my little sister is not here to greet me.

"Faith is over at mom and dad's house tonight. I thought it would be nice if just the two of us got to hang out tonight," my dad says. He is very glad I'm home. "I got some frozen pizza, popcorn and soda for dinner. Then later, after I beat you at rummy a few times we can watch a movie on cable." My father knows what I like to do when I am home. Guy nights are a tradition with us.

I smile and am surprised how nothing has changed. My same old dad, doing the same old things. You just got to love coming home.

The next day, my dad's parents and Faith come over to the house. It's good to see everyone. Faith, my little sister is ten years younger than I am. She is a very energetic twelve year old. She just talks and talks about everything going on in her life. I know she is the bright star that draws my family together. I'm glad to see she is so happy.

My mother's parents come for dinner. The only one missing is my mother, but she really left the family four years ago. I guess I will have to make a trip over to the casino to see her while I am here. From what I gather, she hardly sees Faith anymore. Our grandparents help dad raise Faith. I'm glad they are all still young enough to be involved in her life. I'm not looking forward to the day when my grandparents grow old and die. They have all been like extra parents to me. I'm blessed to have such a family. If Caleb were home, he would be here as well. He was always a part of our family. It saddens me to think of Caleb's spirit trapped and tormented in the Wendigo.

After dinner, I go outside to sit on the porch with my father and two grandfathers. I know they can tell I have something to say. "What I have to tell you is for your ears only. I will try to give you as much detail as I can so you fully understand my story."

I tell them everything that happened when I went to the cabin on Bear Ridge, except the part with me and Liz. I tell them about my fight with the Wendigo and my vision of Grandfather Broken Nose. I even tell them about Agent Johansen and her offer to join her organization. I tell them of my plan to try to kill the Wendigo so I can free Caleb's spirit.

"You all tried to hide it from me but I know you are members of the False Face Society. I wish to join and make my own mask as Grandfather Broken Nose instructed me. I took this for the mask," I say, showing them the part of the Wendigo I scalped off. It's mostly black hair but a little part of it is white. "I think the *blood we share* that Broken Nose spoke of is my blood. We were blood brothers and cousins so I will coat the mask in my own blood," I explain, passing my dad the grisly trophy so they can examine it.

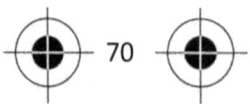

The men look at each other and all nod. My grandfather Amos Longstride is the first to speak. "You have been given a great vision and with it, a great destiny. There are but a few stories of masks of the great beasts being made. This sets you apart from us. We were given visions of healing the people. You are destined to be a hunter. We will help you as we can." He passes me back the Wendigo trophy, having examined it while speaking.

My grandfather Jubal Seneca speaks next. "I agree with Amos. You are destined to live your life with a knife in your hand. I wish you could stay among the people and live contented among us but I saw from a young age that you were restless. Your fate and Caleb's have always been intertwined. One day, I am sure you will face him and only one will walk away."

Then my father speaks. "I am proud of you and honored to call you my son. We will go over the legends and find out what we can of the Wendigo to help you in your fight. Tomorrow we will bring you to the longhouse of Grandfather Broken Nose and you will become one of us. Then you will go on your vision quest to find the tree that calls to you. You may be gone many days so prepare yourself. When you find the right tree, the mask will almost carve itself."

"Thank you all, my fathers. It weighs heavy upon me to burden you with my story but I knew you were the right ones to tell. You have always stood by me," I say, embracing each man in turn.

After everyone heads home and Faith is in bed, I go into Salamanca, the town of around 6000 upon the reservation. I still find it odd that the population of Salamanca is only 1.5% Native American even though it's within the reservation.

I want to stop by the Little Pub, a local restaurant and bar. My family told me that Jessy is back from her sophomore year of college and is working at the Little Pub. Jessy Sky Deer is two years behind me in school. We dated my last two years of high school and pick things up every time we see each other over breaks and during the summers. I dated other girls at college but I keep coming back to Jessy. I haven't seen her in six months and I could sure use a little Jessy time.

The Little Pub is not so little anymore. It added a large restaurant addition a couple of years ago. It is owned by the Little family. The Littles own a couple of liquor stores, some rental property and the Little Pub. They are very well off. There oldest son is Phillip Little and he has been after Jessy for the last couple of years. I don't like that she is now working for him.

The bar side of the Little Pub is starting to pick up but is still pretty slow when I arrive a little after 10. I see Jessy waiting on a couple guys. I sit at a table and watch her.

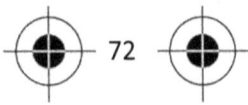

Jessy is a small thing, almost a foot shorter than I am, so a couple inches over five feet. She is as slender as a doe in the early spring after a harsh winter. Her hair is black as night but soft as corn silk. She has cut it since I last saw her. I don't really like it. I'm so used to her having long hair so this will take some getting used to.

Jessy looks over and sees me. Her face lights up with a huge smile, the one that keeps me coming back. She comes over to me and I drink in her bright blue eyes. That is the one part of her that just doesn't fit and betrays her heritage. Her grandmother was a blond, blue-eyed white woman. I don't hold it against her but my grandparents have been pretty vocal about the need to carry on the pureblood Seneca line. I don't think they realize how few options that gives me. On this reservation, the amount of pure blood girls within five years of my age are less than fifty and there is probably no more than a few hundred more in the rest of the world. In the end, I will probably end up disappointing my grandparents and marrying Jessy. It could be a lot worse. I could marry a woman with no Seneca blood at all. I don't see how blood has anything to do with falling in love.

"Hey Logan, when did you get in town?" Jessy smiles at me.

"Last night. I heard you were working up here so I took a chance," I smile back at her, wanting to touch her but knowing it's not a good idea at work.

"Yeah, I just started here. I wanted my job at the paper back but they have cut staff because everyone reads the news online now," Jessy frowns.

"It's good to see you, it has been too long," I say, thinking it has been way too long since I have seen her smile.

"I heard about Caleb. I'm very sorry. I know how close you two were," Jessy sympathizes, putting her hand on my shoulder.

"I don't know if I will ever be over Caleb being gone," I stammer, starting to get a little emotional. Tears sting at the corners of my eyes.

"You going to order something or just gab at the help all night," a voice that I know belongs to Phillip Little comes from behind me.

I turn to face Phillip. He has a smug look on his face that I do not like one bit. I had the chance in high school to beat the crap out of Phillip but I took the high road and let him off easy. Right now, I wish I had beat the snot out of him when I had a chance. Sure I know I could lick him, but this is not the time or place for such a thing. Phillip believes, because his family has money, that makes him better than everyone else. I think it just makes him as little as his name.

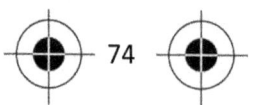

"Hello Phillip," I say, trying to keep anger out of my voice.

"I figure you would be drinking it up like your mom. She almost single handedly keeps us in business," Phillip taunts me.

I get to my feet and Jessy puts her hand on my chest. "Don't let him rile you, Logan. I get off at one, I will see you then," Jessy whispers.

I stare at Phillip and fantasize about punching him in the nose. I nod at Jessy and turn to leave.

"Guess the civilized white man college took all the fight out of ya, huh Logan. At least we have your mom old Sally LongSUCK to laugh at around town,"

I turn and move with purpose towards Phillip. Jessy gets in my way again but I gently brush her aside. Phillip has gone too far. I see excitement and then fear flash across Phillip's eyes. I think he just realized he is in too deep.

I grab him by the shirt and pull him close to me. I then whisper so only he can hear my words. "If you ever talk about my mother again I will take you into the woods and slowly peel your skin off a strip at a time. Then I will curse your spirit, burn your body and scatter the ashes to the four winds so your soul will never find rest."

I let go of Phillip and walk away. As I pass Jessy, I take her in my arms and plant a long wet one on her.

"See you at one," I smile to her before walking out the door.

I drive around town a little just to kill time. I see the sign for the casino and decide I had better get it over with. I haven't seen my mom in almost a year. I hate what has happened to her or more accurately, what she did to herself. When this casino first went in, I was behind it as a way to make money for the tribe. I didn't think I would lose my mom to it. I hate the place now. I realize if it weren't here, my mom would have just found somewhere else to lose herself, but the casino is here and it's easier for me to hate it than my mom.

From experience, I know my best bet of finding mom is to search the bar areas first, then hit the casino floor. I find her at a crap table all over this white haired old geezer. I stand back and watch as she rubs up to the man, trying to hold his attention as he is rolling the dice. She is just trying way too hard and if she wasn't so pretty, I bet this guy would push her away. She is swaying a little and I can tell she is drunk. She caresses the old dude like he is some magic piggy bank that will pop out drugs and booze if she just rubs him hard enough. I can't believe that is my mother. She is hustling guys for money and probably giving them her body in return. I hope someday I can help my mom out of her pit of depression but not tonight. I don't want to even speak

76

to her. After I can stomach no more of watching my mom work her john, I leave.

Jessy comes out of the Little Pub about 1:20am. She walks over to my car and leans in the window. "That fucker Phillip made me stay late to clean up the bathrooms. As long as you are in town, this may turn out to be a hard job to keep. Whatever you said really got to him." Jessy pauses to see if I'm going to comment before continuing. "I need a shower. If you want, you can follow me home," Jessy winks at me.

Jessy lives with her parents in town during the summers when she is home from college. She sneaks me in and we go down stairs. Her parents turned her room into an office and she is stuck on the couch in the basement when she is home. There is a bathroom with a shower in the basement so she does have some privacy.

"Make yourself at home, Logan," Jessy says as she strips off her shirt and heads for the shower.

I take this as an opportunity to follow her into the bathroom. She has her bra on the floor when I enter and covers her breasts with her arms. "Do you mind?" she smirks at me.

"I could use a shower too…" I smile at her wickedly.

She drops her arms and throws them around my neck. We kiss and frantically pull off each other's clothes. We have sex in the bathroom before ever getting in the shower. In the shower, we are both glowing from our recent lovemaking. I lather up my chest and then rub myself all over her body, getting her all soapy. She giggles and we play. I wash her hair and bend down to let her wash mine. It's a fun experience, that is more intimate than sexual.

We towel each other off and I walk out into the basement naked. I open the sleeper bed and pull the mattress onto the floor. I know from experience that the damn things squeaks to high heaven if you move on it even a little, let alone if you try to have sex on it. Jessy comes out with a towel wrapped around her. She walks over to me and I rip her towel off, spinning her around. She giggles and I take her in my arms. She is so small that I can easily carry her around. Being with Jessy has always felt so right.

I lay her on the mattress and kiss my way down her body. I go all the way down to her toes then up between her thighs. She runs her fingers through my damp hair as I use my tongue to make her call my name again and again.

"Make love to me," she whispers when I come up for air.

We make sweet love and fall asleep in each other's arms.

Chapter 8:
False Face Society

The next day I spend in the longhouse of Grandfather Broken Nose learning the secrets of the False Face Society. I meet other members of the society and prepare myself for the journey to find my vision tree. The society is much more than I ever thought. My eyes are opened to many things that I had closed off in my years of living in the modern world.

At sunset, I start my vision quest. I stay awake all night within the longhouse, meditating on the mask I've been called to make. I call and dance for Grandfather Broken Nose to guide me. As the sun rises, I set out on my vision quest to find the tree that holds the mask of the Wendigo.

I wander the woods of our reservation and beyond for the next week. I live off the land, eating and sleeping little. On the tenth night, I lose my footing and tumble down into a hollow. I am bruised a little but suffer no major injuries. Nestled in the side of the hollow is a gnarled ancient tree. Its bark is almost black and crawls with ants. The whole area smells of death and decay. I know this is the tree.

I move around it, examining the tree. I feel the tree, looking for the right place to carve the mask. A sharp piece of bark slices my hand and my blood drips upon the spot. This is where I will carve my mask. I take out Enuk's knife and under the full moon begin to carve the mask of the Wendigo.

Minutes ago, I was weary to the point of collapse from lack of food and sleep. Now I'm invigorated and the mask carves itself. I go into a trance as I slice into the living gnarled old tree. Enuk's knife slices paper-thin strips off the tree over and over as the mask begins to take shape. I work hour after hour until the dawn comes and the newly risen sun reveals the mask of the Wendigo. I'm startled by how much it looks like Caleb. It is Caleb, but with skin pulled tight over his skull. Its teeth are sharp and bestial. It's the Wendigo.

I cover the mask in my blood before I cut it out of the tree. My blood seems to be absorbed into the mask as fast as I apply it. With mask in hand, I set off to the longhouse of Old Broken Nose. I'm surprised that for all my wandering I am able to make it back before dark. I wandered for ten days and came to a place that was near where I started.

My grandfathers and father greet me when I return. I can see relief wash over their sober faces

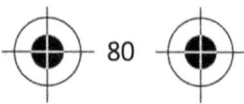

when they see me. I had been gone so long they were very worried for me. I go into the longhouse and curl up with my mask to get some much needed sleep.

The next day, I work alone to finish the mask. I only paint it with my own blood, which turns it black. I put the hair of the Wendigo on it. I tie a pouch of tobacco in it's hair as a payment to the mask for it's service. I also make white corn mush myself and place it before the mask as payment.

The next night, I show my mask of the Wendigo to the other members of the False Face Society and don it for the first time. Everyone puts on their masks and we all dance around a fire. I sit alone at first as the entire group dance around me with turtle shell rattles and they blow smoke over me. When all have had their turn, I put on my mask. I feel a burning on my face that soon flows through my body. I am clothed only in a loincloth. The scar on my left shoulder begins to burn and blood runs from it. I scream out in pain from the Wendigo's wound. My body is hot. I feel like I'm going to burn up. I can tell what is happening to me is not normal. The others gather around me shaking their turtle rattles and blowing smoke at me. Blood continues to run from my wound and I writhe on the floor in agony. My whole body is wracked with pain.

My grandfather Amos tries to take off my mask but is burned when he touches it. The men do not

know what to do so they do what they know and
continue to dance around me calling upon
Grandfather Broken Nose to help me. I do not
remember much of what happened that night. I was
wracked with pain until the sun rose. The men all
chanted, danced, shook their rattles and blew tobacco
smoke over me all night. Some of the men collapsed
from exhaustion. As the morning sun rose, my mask
fell off my face.

I sleep through the day right where I fell. When I
awake shortly after sunset, my father and
grandfathers are there. They stare at me as if I am
some strange thing to be studied from afar.

"Logan, are you all right?" my father asks.

I'm surprised at how good I feel. "I'm fine.
Actually, I feel renewed."

"Do you know what happened?" My father asks,
a concerned look in his eyes. He looks older today,
more haggard and weary.

"When I put on the mask I felt hot and a great
pain shot through my body. I kept seeing visions of
the Wendigo. I think it felt the pain as I did. I think we
are truly connected now." I reveal not even knowing
what I said had happened until it passed my lips. Part
of me touched the Wendigo when I put the mask on. I
became it and it became me. I think I gained some of
its power when that happened. Then I realize
something. "I can sense the Wendigo now, but I think

it can also sense me. It's hunting me. It will probably take weeks but if I stay here, it will come here. I must leave before it gets too close."

"We will speak of you leaving later. For now, let's consider what happened when you had the mask on," my father says, pausing for a moment before continuing. "Your mask would not come off, your shoulder bled and your mask changed," my father tells me looking very serious.

"I remember my arm bleeding. How did my mask change?" I wonder, touching my shoulder where the scar is.

My father gets my mask. It's on a tray when he brings it to me. I think they are all afraid to touch it. When I made my mask, I smeared blood all over it that it seemed to soak up. The blood turned it black. It is now the ash grey skin color of the Wendigo.

"We think the blood went into you," Grandfather Amos says, leaning down to examine the mask.

"That could be right. I felt hot and the pain was unbearable. Is this how it was when you all made your masks?" I ask, but know by their faces the answer before they speak.

"No one in the Society has ever seen a reaction like yours. No one can even remember stories of such a thing happening." Jubal says quietly looking around. "A few of the men want to cast you out of the Society. They claim that Broken Nose has cursed you," Grandfather Jubal says, looking angry at the suggestion.

"Oh…well…um…what do you all think?" I ask, unsure and looking to my father figures.

"We still feel you have been chosen by Old Broken Nose to be a hunter. You will live and die by the knife. We know of the Wendigo and the details of your vision. This gives us knowledge that the others do not have. The three of us have discussed it and do not think you should share your story with the others or anyone else for that matter," Grandfather Amos says.

"I thank all of you for your confidence. I admit I don't really know what is going on. I do know I feel pretty good but am damn hungry. Can we get something to eat?" I ask, getting to my feet.

"Hahaha," my dad laughs. "Well he sure acts like the same old Logan, thinking about his stomach first." The men laugh and I'm glad they are no longer so serious, even if the joke is at my expense.

We go over to my father's house. My grandmothers start preparing a grand meal for all of us. My father waited for me at the longhouse of Old Broken Nose all ten days while I was on my vision quest. My grandfathers were there most of the time but took turns keeping the rest of the family up to date. I hear that Jessy stopped by the house a couple times looking for me and I've orders to call her as soon as I can.

I call Jessy on the phone. "Hey Jessy, sorry I've been out of touch," I apologize.

"I heard you were out in the woods with your dad and grandfathers. How did all that male bonding go?" She teases.

"It was good. You want to stop by, or want me to come over?"

"I'll be right over. Am I invited to dinner?"

"Sure come on over," I reply, just wanting to see her.

My grandparent's eyes move between Jessy and me throughout dinner. I know they all like her but consider she is not good enough for me. It's kind of awkward but Jessy is used to it. She understands their slight prejudice. We have talked about it many times.

After dinner, we hang out and split into groups. The women all clear the table and go into the kitchen. The men go on the porch to smoke, drink and talk. None of my family drinks or smokes much, especially since my mom became an alcoholic. But they do know how to talk.

"Can you sense the Wendigo now?" My father asks.

I concentrate for a minute. "No, nothing. I don't know how it works. I just know that when I wore the mask I could feel and see everything it was doing."

"Maybe you should try on the mask and see if that helps," Grandfather Amos suggests.

I nod my head and go get the Wendigo mask. I put it on but nothing happens at all. There is no pain, vision or sensation of any kind. I take the mask off and wrap it back up in cloth. "Sorry, nothing," I say, disappointed.

"There has to be something. What happened to you when you put on that mask was true magic. It must have changed you as it changed your mask," Grandfather Jubal says staring at me.

I get up and walk along the porch and into the woods. I walk pretty far before I realize I can see everything almost as if it is daylight. I sniff the air and can pick out a distinct smell for all the people in the house as well as many different animals in the area. I track different scents to a squirrel perched on a branch and a raccoon in a bush.

I try to climb up a tree to see if I can catch the squirrel because I think the Wendigo could have done it. It's hard going and I slip. I would have fallen but my fingertips and toes are so strong I'm almost able to run up the tree.

I run back to the house to tell my fathers what I've discovered and notice that I can run much faster than before. I leap up over the railing of the porch and land crouched next to my very startled father.

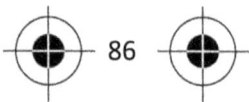

My grandfathers look at me as if I'm something to be feared. I can even smell a little of their fright and wish I could not. I don't ever want my family to have reason to fear me.

I spring to the roof and then into a tree top over forty feet away. My fathers watch me. I jump down upon the porch and stand before them.

"I've changed, as you can see. Grandfather Broken Nose has given me the powers I will need to kill the Wendigo," I boast, feeling proud.

"Son, you must never show anyone else what you just showed us. You should not show off. These gifts are sacred. They were given to you for a purpose. We of the False Face Society live in anonymity because we serve the people. We do not seek fame or worship for what we can do. You must hide your gifts from others and only use them when necessary. With great magic, comes great responsibility," Grandfather Amos says, looking very seriously at me.

I bow my head ashamed. I admit that I'm happy and proud to have these gifts but I see the wisdom in what Amos says. "I will do as you say grandfather. I thank you for your wisdom."

"Amos does not mean to scold you. You need to go alone in the woods and learn your gifts as well as you can, for you will need them when you face the Wendigo. Old Broken Nose gave this vision and purpose to you alone. It is you who must carry this great boon and secret. You have honored us by sharing your secret with us," Grandfather Jubal says.

"We are not saying you must face the Wendigo alone, just that you should not reveal your secrets to others. We are your family and will stand by you. Just be sure you can trust anyone you would reveal these secrets to," my father says.

"Your wisdom is very welcome. I thank you all," I say, meaning it very much.

We talk for a while and they tell me every tidbit they have ever heard about the Wendigo. After a while Amos has something interesting to offer. "I don't believe you need your mask to use your powers. Everything you just showed us you did with it wrapped up over here on the table. When you first put it on in the longhouse of Broken Nose, I think you took some of the magic of the Wendigo. You should have your gifts as long as the Wendigo lives," Grandfather Amos says.

"I think Amos may be right about this. Just as you and Caleb are tied together now you and the Wendigo share a connection. The mask may be what binds that connection. If it is destroyed, your connection may be lost. You should keep it safe and secret," Grandfather Jubal agrees.

"I think I should take the mask of the Wendigo with me just in case, but you may be right. I will keep it hidden away," I agree.

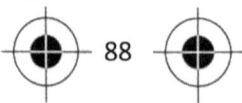

"What are you going to do about this monster hunting group you talked to us about?" Grandfather Amos asks.

"I'm not sure. If I could work with them and not for them, they could probably help me a lot in hunting the Wendigo. I do want to keep my secrets, as you suggested, and be able to walk away when it's over," I say, worrying about how I might do that if I joined this secret organization.

"This woman you describe is like a snake. Beautiful, graceful, and possible to handle when care is taken, but if you agitate her, she will turn on you and sink her deadly fangs into you. I suggest caution when dealing with her," Grandfather Jubal recommends.

"So you are not against me contacting Agent Johansson?" I ask.

"No, but heed Jubal's warning. No matter what you are told, once you jump into a pit of vipers, it can be much harder to climb out than it was to get in," Grandfather Amos says.

"You know our tribe's saying about those who do great things. He who would do great things should not attempt them all alone," my father adds.

"I will remember your wisdom," I say.

We talk for a little while more before my grandparents all head home. Jessy and Faith hang out with me until it's time for Faith to go to bed. I put

Faith to bed and help my father get out of his wheelchair and into bed. Then it's just Jessy and me.

Jessy and I go out back and walk into the woods. My senses are alive. I can see, hear and smell everything. I get all distracted with the new sensations. Jessy squeezes my hand to get my attention. I realize we have walked a mile into the woods already.

Jessy looks up at me. "Where are your thoughts, Logan?"

"I'm sorry I was just thinking about what my father and grandfather were talking to me about."

"Oh…were they lecturing you on marring a pure blooded Seneca again?" Jessy grumbles, getting annoyed.

"No it's not that. I joined the False Face Society." I know I'm not supposed to tell anyone, but Jessy is my best friend now that Caleb is gone. I just need someone else to talk to.

"Oh, so how'd that go?" She asks, but I can tell she is thinking, why the hell did you do that!

"I know I'm really young and it seems rushed. I actually had a dream from Grandfather Broken Nose. I know we used to make fun of people who claimed to have visions and do magic, but I've seen it for real," I say, kind of getting carried away in the moment.

"Are you all right, Logan? You think you actually experienced real magic?" Jessy questions, with a very skeptical look on her face.

"Yes, real magic. It all started when I went looking for Caleb. Just believe me when I tell you that at least some of our legends are true."

"What are you talking about? Either tell me or don't. I don't want to listen to all this vague bullshit," Jessy snaps, turning to stalk away from me. She walks a little ways away and sits on a stump, glaring at me.

I stop to think about Jessy. Do I trust her like I do my father and grandfathers? I cock my head a little bit and stare at her. She does have a little of a temper but she has always stood by me. How will she take the news? Umm, well that is another thing. I don't think she will freak out or anything. She might think I'm crazy, but I think she can handle it. She never has been a gossip so I can't see her telling my secret.

"Jessy, you are my best friend and I love you. I'm not ready to get married but when I am I will probably ask you."

Jessy looks surprised, her eyes wide with shock. "Well I'm not sure how to respond to that, you idiot," Jessy says walking up to me and shoving me back a little. "Where the hell did that come from?" she asks but then continues. "You know I love you. And yes, I've thought about marrying you," she admits, giving me a gracious smile and taking my hand in hers.

"Oh God, Jess, I didn't mean to piss you off. I just have some really heavy shit going on right now and I want to share it with you. I wanted to let you know how I felt about you I guess. The stuff I need to tell you is life changing. You up for that?" I ask, watching how she reacts.

"Life changing, how? Like you want to move in together, or magic is real?" she asks, pulling me down to sit next to her on a log.

"Like proof magic is real. I'm not joking, so really think about it. Do you want your life changed that much?" I ask, jumping up and raking my fingers through my hair. I pace back and forth like a trapped animal.

I can tell Jessy doesn't really believe me. "Just tell me."

"I think you will do better by seeing, rather than hearing," I wonder, if what I'm about to do is totally insane. Oh, well, in for a penny...

I crouch down and leap thirty feet onto a tree limp above Jessy. Her jar drops open. I leap from tree to tree and then back next to her.

After a moment, Jessy catches her breath enough to speak. "How in the hell did you do that?" she shrieks, jumping up and backing away from me slightly.

"When I went to Alaska, I encountered a real Wendigo. It nearly killed me. In a vision Grandfather

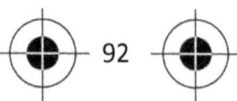

Broken Nose asked me to make a mask of the Wendigo so that I could hunt it. That is what I've been doing in the woods. The mask I made of the Wendigo gave me these powers," I reveal to Jessy, reaching out toward her. I hope what I've done has not completely scared her away.

"Really?" Do others of the False Face Society have these powers?" she asks, starting to relax a little, but still looking slightly stunned.

"No, they had never seen anything like what happened to me. When I put on the mask, it burned and hurt me. It would not come off. Many of the False Face members are scared of me now and they do not even know what powers the mask gave me. I've only told my father, grandfathers and you. I don't intend to tell anyone else." I carefully take a couple of steps forward and am thankful Jessy does not back away again.

"Wow, that's a hell of a thing to lay on a girl?"

"I'm sorry Jessy. I just needed someone to talk to beside old men."

"It's alright, Logan. I'm honored you felt you could tell me," Jessy says as she comes up to give me a hug. I wrap my arms around her and breathe in her clean scent. The familiar smell comforts me. I'm reluctant to end our embrace.

We spend the next hour just talking about everything. It feels so good just to hang out with Jessy. We go back to my house and go to my bedroom. We make love and fall asleep holding each other.

Chapter 9:
Goodbyes

I spend the next couple of days with Jessy and my family. I keep looking at the phone Agent Johansson gave me, wondering if I should call her. I finally decide I need to hear what she has to say so I push the speed dial and listen to it ring.

"Yes," answers a sexy sounding female voice on the other end of the line.

"Agent Johansson?"

"Logan, it is good to hear from you. What can I do for you?" Agent Johansson says, in her confident business voice. Damn, she knew I would call.

"My personal business is finished. I'm ready to go on that hunting trip we discussed."

"Good. Shall I make the arrangements to pick you up?" Agent Johansson asks, and I can hear her pen scratching on paper.

"Um…ok but I want it understood that we are working together and that I do not work for you," I say, trying to be clear from the very beginning. I know if I don't establish some control now, I never will with this woman.

"Sure, Logan whatever you say. I will text you with directions. Meet me there at 9 am tomorrow," Agent Johansson says and then disconnects without even giving me time to say ok. I've a feeling we will have to hash out the conditions of my employment again.

I pack and tell my family and Jessy I'm leaving. Jessy calls in sick to work so she can spend the night with me. I hang out with my family the rest of the day. Only my father, grandfathers and Jessy know why I'm really going away. Everyone else thinks I have another hunting guide job up north.

Jessy and I take a couple of blankets into the woods after everyone is in bed. I've learned that I'm much stronger than I used to be and need to be careful not to hurt Jessy when we have sex. A couple of days ago, I bruised her when I was on top. Tonight we make love under the stars like we used to when we wanted to have sex in high school. We would just slip into the woods with some blankets. This night brings back all those fond memories.

"I know you see other girls sometimes when you are away, hell I've dated other guys in college. But I want you to know that I will always love you no matter who we end up with. You were my first lover and dearest to my heart," Jessy confesses while she is on top of me. I can see tears in her eyes and I know she is afraid for me.

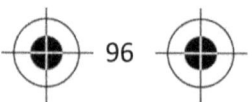

"I love you too Jessy. I promise I will be ok and I will come back," I vow as she slumps to my chest, sobbing.

"I don't want you to die. I couldn't stand it if you died," Jessy says as she weeps on top of me.

I'm not sure what to do. Jessy is losing it. I know neither of us wants to spend our last night together crying. I roll her on her back and lean over her. My hard attention focuses her back to the moment. I kiss her and whisper. "I'm here now. Love me, Jessy. Just love me tonight." She focuses on having sex and we enjoy being together. She falls asleep after, so I carry her back to the house. I snuggle up next to her in my bed and go to sleep.

Chapter 10: Nightmare

The moon is half-full and the night air very cold. I can smell the lake up ahead through the trees. Constant pains come from my gut. Sometimes the pain is so much it makes me cry out. I have to eat again soon. The pain is unbearable. I must find food.

I stop dead in my tracks and slowly sweep my head from side to side, trying to catch a scent. The fresh smell of my prey fills my nostrils. The scent is sweet and clean smelling. My nose leads the way as I pick up speed and bound through the woods. The scent grows stronger and becomes mixed with other scents. There is at least three of my prey up ahead. They will sate my hunger pains for a little while. I need to eat more and more to be even a little satisfied.

A clearing comes into view. Beyond the woods, out in the open sits the home of my prey. Large, white and on wheels. My meal awaits within. I want to circle the meadow for signs of danger but my hunger pains almost bend me over. My need to feed is what drives me.

I dash across the open ground and move to the door of the RV. The handle turns in my grey-clawed hands. I step inside and see a picture on the counter. A man, woman and five-year old girl. The picture matches the scents I've been following. Creeping down the hallway, I enter the main bedroom. The man and woman cling to each other under the covers, unaware I'm here. Pain shoots through me and I know I must feed on their flesh. I leap upon the bed ripping and clawing into their flesh. Their screams fill my ears…

"Logan...Logan, wake up," a voice yells at me.

I open my eyes and Jessy is shaking me violently trying to wake me. "I'm awake," I say, trying to understand what just happened.

Jessy's eyes are filled with terror and concern. Sweat covers my body and there is blood on the sheets. The blood is from my left shoulder scar, where the Wendigo clawed me. The wound looks fresh and bloody as if it just happened.

"BAM, BAM, BAM," comes from the door. "Logan, are you okay?" Faith screams, her voice frantic with fear.

"I'm ok, Faith. It was just a nightmare. Go tell dad everything is ok and go back to bed. I'm sorry I woke you." I feel terrible that I disturbed the whole house.

"What happened, Logan? You were howling like nothing I've ever heard," Jessy demands to know.

"I saw and felt everything the Wendigo was doing. It was as if I was inside its body but had no control. I felt what it felt," I mutter, trying to figure this out even as I'm saying it.

"What was it doing?" Jessy whispers, almost not wanting to know.

"It tracked and killed a family. It was so hungry and was going to eat…" I stop as I see the look of horror on Jessy's face.

"Maybe it was just a nightmare."

"Look at my arm. Something magical just happened to me," I say, as I get up and wipe the blood off my arm with a t-shirt.

Jessy sits on the bed watching me. She has the sheet pulled up around her, but otherwise she is naked as I am. I don't like her look of fear mixed with concern. I look away and pull on a pair of shorts. "I need to take a shower. I'll be back in a few," I offer as I open the door and walk down the hall.

The hot shower feels good. My fresh wound is rapidly healing to the scar I had when I went to sleep a couple of hours ago. My connection to the Wendigo is strong. I think about what I saw and try to figure out where the Wendigo was. The forest looked more like Canada than Alaska. The Wendigo is moving south into more populated areas and closer to me.

The vision of Jessy staring at me with alarm, as if she had never seen me before haunts me. Will things

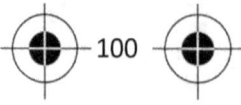

ever be the same between us again? Maybe she would be better off without me. My hunt for the Wendigo could take months or even years. Every night she will wonder if I am still alive. If I do die, we are not legally connected in any way so she will not be as involved in the families mourning. I have placed her in a sort of limbo with half promises of a future that may never come. How did things get so complicated?

When I go back to bed, I find that Jessy has changed the sheets. She is waiting for me under the covers. I crawl in next to her and hold her tight. Neither of us speaks. We clutch each other tight knowing this may be the last night we spend together. Finally sleep comes.

The next morning I don't have a lot of time before I have to leave. I tell my dad all about the dream and how it made my shoulder bleed. He mostly nods his head and looks concerned. I say my goodbyes to Faith. Jessy walks me out to my car.

"Take care of yourself, Logan," Jessy says trying to smile but I can tell it's forced. She is sad I'm going away and afraid I will never come back. I know she wants me to stay but I'm glad she doesn't ask me to forgo my quest. I would be too tempted to stay.

"I don't know what the future is going to bring anymore, Jess. Live your life and be happy," I say, holding her face in my hands.

"What are you saying?" Jessy demands, backing away.

"Just that I don't know when I can call or will be back. You don't have to wait for me. I want you to be happy."

Jessy slaps me across the face and then pounds her fists into my chest. "Damn you Logan. I'm happy when I am with you." She starts to cry but stops herself and looks up at me. "You better come back or that Wendigo will not be the only one hunting you down," she vows, and I can tell she means it.

"I love you too," I smile, giving her a light kiss.

Jessy truly smiles at me and I can see her love for me in those bright blue eyes of hers. "Sometimes I wish I didn't love you, but God help me I do. Take care of yourself Logan."

We kiss and hug tightly. I really have to leave now or I'll be late. We wave to each other as I drive off to meet Agent Johansson.

Chapter 11:
The Hunt Begins

It takes me forty minutes to arrive where I'm supposed to meet Agent Johansson. The place is a rundown strip motel off the main road. It has twelve units and appears to be closed for good. I pull in to wait.

At 9am, my phone rings. "Drive your car around back," the inviting voice of Agent Johansson orders. Then the line goes dead. I've never been hung up on so many times by a woman. Not sure I like it.

I drive around back of the motel. There is a black Lexus in back so I park next to it. Agent Johansson rolls down her window when I pull next to her. "Leave your keys under the seat. Put your bags in my backseat and hop in," Agent Johansson commands.

I do as I'm told but I don't like leaving my car here. It's not much of a car but it's all I have. Agent Johansson drives off after I get in and fasten my seatbelt. She is wearing a black suit, but the skirt is a little short. I can see her legs well up past the knee. She does have nice legs. Her jacket is a little tight and opens at her bust line. I can see the tops of her large breasts. Her blond hair is up in a bun without a hair

out of place. I wonder how she does that? Maybe all
her years of government training. She has her
sunglasses on and a shade of lipstick that seems too
vibrant for government work. I'm even more
convinced that if Agent Johansson really let her hair
down and showed off her figure, she would stop
traffic. She is a damn fine looking woman.

Agent Johansson watches the road and doesn't
talk or look at me. I bet she is aware of me checking
her out but does not even glance at me. When we turn
a corner, I notice a ring on her right ring finger. It's a
diamond ring, like you would get for an engagement,
but it is on the wrong hand. The stone is not large but
not too small either. Someone from the middle class
might buy something like this when they wanted to
get married. I wonder if Agent Johansson was
engaged once. Maybe she kept the ring and still wears
it to remind her not to get trapped in a relationship.
She doesn't look like the relationship type. More like
the rock your world, then you wake up handcuffed in
some hotel somewhere never to see her again, type. I
get a little excited just thinking about it. I squirm in
my seat to make sure my arousal is not noticeable.

Agent Johansson pulls down a gravel road and
parks in pretty much the middle of nowhere. I can't
see any buildings or hear any cars go by. Agent
Johansson gets out of the car and motions for me to
do the same. She walks around to the trunk and opens

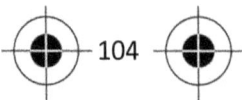

104

it. She gets out what I think are metal detecting wands or maybe bug detection devices. She goes over every inch of me with those wands. Sometimes they brush my skin and send a little shiver through me. I can't help it but this kind of turns me on. Agent Johansson uses her hands to feel under my arms and between my legs. She can't help to notice my arousal. She is resting back on her heels, squatting in front of me with her hand in my crotch. She grasps my hard cock and feels around it without even looking up at me. Damn, she is one cool chick.

When she is done with me, she goes through my entire luggage. She finds nothing, so we get back into the car and continue down the road. We drive out to a small airfield and a private jet is waiting for us. We get on the plane and take off. There is a pilot, copilot and two other people who I assume are agents, on the plane. Agent Johansson and I sit in the back of the plane at a sort of booth alone.

"Last night a family of three was killed," Agent Johansson flips a copy of the same picture the Wendigo looked at when it went into the RV on the table in front of me. "Their flesh was torn from their bodies. The local authorities are calling it an attack by a pack of wolves. We are heading to the area to investigate."

I get a sick feeling in my stomach. I was inside the Wendigo when it found that family. I saw this very picture through its eyes. They look so happy in the photo. I witnessed the Wendigo stalk them and tear into the parents. I knew it was real and not a nightmare but to have it confirmed like this makes it violently authentic.

"Are you all right Logan? You look sick."

"I'll be fine. Could I get a drink?"

Agent Johansson gets up and walks over to a bar area close by. She fills two glasses full of ice. She fills them both with straight bourbon and comes back to the table. She takes a good swig of her drink. I take a small sip of mine. It has to be around noon, which is definitely too early for me to start drinking. The sharp taste of the bourbon shocks me back to the issues at hand.

"If I get you to the scene, do you think you can track Caleb?" Agent Johansson asks.

I'm shocked when she calls it Caleb. "It is a Wendigo!" I insist.

"Ok, do you think you can track the Wendigo?"

"I will sure try."

"I gather bullets did not harm it very much. What would you recommend we use?"

"Fire. It was definitely afraid of fire."

"We have mini flame throwers called Blasters. They should give us an advantage," Agent Johansson offers, making notes on her phone as we talk.

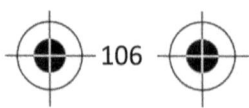

"How many people do we have to hunt the Wendigo?" I ask, noticing how her blouse drops down when she bends over slightly to work on her phone. This gives me an amazing view of her ample breasts.

"A four man fire team plus me and you. We can get more but I think a small team would be better. What do you think?" Agent Johansson asks, still typing away on her phone.

"How have the men been trained? Do they know the woods?"

"They have all had military training, special ops and recon. They know how to cover and conceal in any environment. They have also been briefed about the Wendigo and understand that such creatures are real. They are all good men," Agent Johansson assures me, not looking up as she talks.

"This thing is damn fast, resistant to damage and smart. It will not be an easy hunt."

"I'm more concerned with it hunting us. If we can choose our place of engagement, I think we'll be ok, but if we are ambushed, then it will be an entirely different matter," Agent Johansson says, finally looking up from her work to study me.

My eyes move from her cleavage to her eyes as they watch me. I know she saw me staring at her but she doesn't show any reaction. She is the calmest chick I have ever met but I wonder if she is all suit and office with no time in the deep woods. "Are you up for this?"

"I can hold my own," Agent Johansson assures me and from the look in her eye, I bet she can. She could probably stare the Wendigo into submission.

One of the men from the front of the plane brings us sandwiches for lunch. We eat and talk about procedures in the field. After lunch, Agent Johansson goes over the weapons we'll be using. She explains the earpieces they use to keep in contact with each other. It's cool to have all this spy stuff to use. With a little plug in my ear, I can hear everything the rest of the team says and talk to them. It's crazy cool.

We end up landing at some small airport in the middle of nowhere Canada. There are two black SUVs waiting for us along with the four-man fire team. Our gear is loaded into the SUV's back but it's obvious that a lot of equipment is already in them. I'm only introduced to one man who leads the fire team known as the Hounds of HEL. His name is Scott but I'm not sure if that is his first or last name.

Agent Johansson and I take one SUV. We follow the Hounds, who are all in the other vehicle. It's clear to me that Agent Johansson is in charge of the operation. We travel an hour before arriving at the crime scene a little before dusk.

I'm startled when I see the white RV. The memories of me in the Wendigo's body haunt me as I

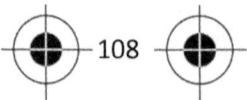

look over the area. Less than twenty hours ago, the Wendigo was here and I saw what it saw. I wonder if he ever sees what I see? Did it see me with Jessy, making love in the woods? That image disturbs me too much to dwell upon it.

We all get out and Agent Johansson moves to take control of the situation. She identifies herself as a Royal Canadian Police Inspector and seems to have all the proper identification. So now I've seen her as an FBI agent and a RCP Inspector. I wonder how many more badges she has up her sleeve.

The locals back off and our team heads in. Three of the Hounds roam the area with weapons, safety off. Agent Johansson, Scott and I head over to the RV. I catch the scent of the Wendigo almost immediately. My heightened senses allow me to follow the scent. I don't want to see that butchered family so I walk off, following the scent. I go to the edge of the clearing and find a clawed human footprint.

"Are you all right, sir?" comes the voice of one of the Hounds right behind me, startling the hell out of me.

"Tell Agent Johansson I have found tracks."

Soon Agent Johansson, Scott and the three Hounds are by my side. "It went this way," I assure them, pointing off into the woods.

Agent Johansson thinks for just a moment then decides what we will do. "It has almost a day's head start and it's getting dark. Logan can you track this thing at night?"

I sniff into the air and know I can see very well in the dark but am not sure about the rest of them. "Yeah, I'm pretty sure I can."

"Scott, have one of the Hounds take an SUV and follow us as best they can by road. The rest of us will gear up and head out," Agent Johansson orders.

Backpacks, night vision goggles, utility belts, combat knives, Blasters and automatic weapons are given to each of us. I leave the night vision goggles as I can see in the dark ever since I put on the Wendigo's mask. I still have Enuk's knife but take the one I'm offered as an extra.

Agent Johansson climbs out of the other SUV in full camo gear. I didn't think she even owned a pair of pants until now. Her hair is down and it shines like gold in the last rays of the sun. I watch her as she flips her hair around and puts it up in a ponytail. She may have fatigues and combat boots on but she is still all kinds of sexy. She straps on her knife and slings her rifle like an expert.

We head out with me at point and Scott brings up the rear. I go at a brisk pace so soon I hear, "slow your pace Logan," in my ear mic.

I'm tracking by smell more than anything. If I can do this, so can the Wendigo. Damn me for not preparing better for this. I'm going along with Agent

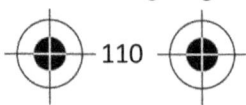

Johansson and have not been thinking about what I would do. We all smell like humans, which is a scent the Wendigo is especially attuned to. If I were prepared, I would have some animal scent to put on us. Maybe it's not too late. "Wait here, I will be right back," I say and run into the woods.

"Logan…Logan, get back to the group," Agent Johansson insists.

I ignore her and close on the deer scent I had smelled. I use my speed to run up and leap onto the deer. I slit its throat. I thank the spirits for giving me this bounty and ask them to forgive my wastefulness. I cut out the mostly full bladder and head back to the group.

"We need to mask our scent. This deer urine will do that. Everyone needs to dribble some on their clothes," I say, standing there with the bloody deer bladder in my hand.

Agent Johansson steps forward and lets me drip deer urine all over her. The others follow suit. I accidently splash one of the Hound's bare arms. "Oh man, it's still warm!" he protests, but doesn't try to wipe it away.

After I'm done scenting everyone including myself, I walk around smelling them. When I catch even the slightest human scent, I put some more urine on them. Agent Johansson needs the most as she is wearing perfume. I know Agent Johansson must hate this but she makes no sign of any discomfort. She is amazingly calm and focused.

I pick up the Wendigo's scent and we continue on. It's totally dark and our pace is slow. I seldom see a track and have to rely on my sense of smell.

We stop for a ten-minute break every two hours. There is no chatter on the mics, as everyone is too focused on not stumbling in the dark to talk. After six hours of walking, I hear the sound of wind wailing through a canyon and I know it's really the Wendigo howling. "That wailing sound is the howl of the Wendigo. We are getting close," I warn the others over my mic.

"Rover, how far out are you?" Agent Johansson asks.

"Twelve klicks to the east ma'am," the Hound in the SUV responds.

"We are heading south. Try to find a way to get closer to us in the next three klicks south," Agent Johansson orders.

"Will do ma'am," the SUV Hound responds and signs off.

We keep following the trail. The wind is from the west so our scent is not being blown directly at the Wendigo, but we are not in the best situation. We should take the time to circle around to the east and come in that direction. The Wendigo would be hard pressed to catch our scent that way. We mostly smell

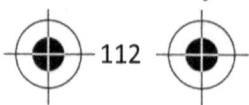

like a group of deer, but every advantage will be important.

I consider talking to Agent Johansson about my plan to circle around but decide against it. I know it's the best course of action and they are following me. I'm pretty sure she would go along with my idea but I don't want to chance it. I veer us off to the east so we can approach the Wendigo from up wind. The smell the corrupting death scent of the Wendigo grows stronger. We are getting close, real close. "We should have contact soon," I whisper into my mic.

I keep swinging us out to the east, then more south. I can smell the Wendigo strongly now. I know it's downwind of us to the west. I go into true hunter mode and move slowly without sound. I move several steps then stop to listen and scan the area. I do this repeatedly as I hunt my prey.

"Found a road heading east. I am five klicks from you and closing," the SUV Hound squawks in our ears.

I creep a little forward and stop to look around. I see a flash of light way off in the distance and figure it's the SUV. "He is heading right for the Wendigo and must have been spotted by now," I say into my mic.

"Slow down and proceed with caution, Rover," Agent Johansson orders.

"Will do ma'am," the roving Hound in the SUV responds.

I continue to creep forward paying close attention to my surroundings. The animal sounds have all but stopped. They can sense the presence of the Wendigo. The night is cold but the wind has died away. The Wendigo must be close.

I come up over a rise and see the SUV coming this way. It rolls to a stop. "End of the line, ma'am. GPS shows me two klicks east of your position. What are your orders?" the Hound in the SUV asks.

"Sit tight and be on guard. The Wendigo is in the area," Agent Johansson commands.

We move slowly forward hunting for any movement. The scent is strong and it's hard to determine exact distance other than it is close. We move on a few steps and then stop to listen and watch. I know the Wendigo must have seen the SUV. I think the SUV is bait for the Wendigo at this point.

I turn and look at Agent Johansson. She is watching the SUV. Right then I realize she is using the Hound inside that vehicle as bait. She has to know that the Wendigo must be coming in for the kill by now. I have to say that is pretty sick, but what choice do we have? We have to lure it out but my conscience forces me to warn the SUV driver.

"Rover be aware the Wendigo will most likely attack you," I say into my mic.

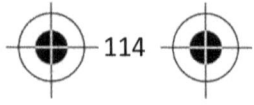

"Roger that," the Hound responds.

I glance back over at Agent Johansson expecting her to be upset but she is still watching the SUV. I just can't figure her out. She is just so calm and collected, like she feels nothing.

We need to approach the SUV so we can offer support if an attack comes. I press on ahead, moving, then stopping to listen repeatedly, as we slowly close on the SUV.

About a klick out, the silence is broken by a "SMASH...SMASH...SMASH," from the SUV's vicinity.

"I have contact. The bullet proof glass is holding but beginning to crack," the Hound in the SUV reports.

"Activate electrical countermeasures," Agent Johansson orders.

As we all move forward, we can see the Wendigo standing on the driver's side beating on the window. Then the SUV erupts in an electrical storm. Thousands of small lightning bolts arch from the vehicle to the Wendigo. "WaaaEee!" the Wendigo screams as it's thrown back from the SUV.

"Report!" Agent Johansson demands.

"Contact has been thrown into the underbrush. I do not have eyes on contact. It could be lying in the brush or mobile," the Hound reports.

"Damn! Use your searchlight to try and spot it. We are closing in," Agent Johansson commands.

I move us forward cautiously but not near as slowly as before. I know the Wendigo is pretty far ahead of us. As we move the SUV's spot light flashes around looking for the Wendigo's body. When we are about half a klick out, the Hound in the SUV reports. "I have no eyes on contact. It's gone, ma'am."

I stop and listen. I take the time to look all around. I can smell the foul odor of death and decay. There is also a strong smell of burnt hair and flesh. The Wendigo has to be almost on top of us. This thought makes me look up and I lock eyes with the Wendigo perched on a limb above Agent Johansson about forty feet away. As I stare at it, I whisper into my mic. "Wendigo is in the tree above Agent Johansson."

I'm amazed that Agent Johansson makes no action to look up or move away. She remains perfectly still while Scott does his job.

"Concentrate fire on one, two, three," Scott says, right before an explosion of automatic weapon fire fills the air. "POP...POP...POP!" The popping sounds of the guns obliterate all other sound for a moment.

"WaaaEee!" the Wendigo screams, as it leaps to the ground and is off into the cover of the woods almost instantly.

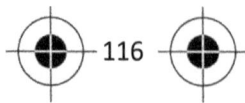

Damn that thing is fast. I walk over to where it fled and contemplate running after it. My eyes scan the forest for movement. The air is thick with the smell of gunpowder so I will not be able to smell the Wendigo if it circles back. Right then I know it will come back. It's hungry and the pains of it's wounds are nothing to the hunger pains it feels. I know this from when I was within the Wendigo in my vision. It has to come back for us, to feed. "It's coming back. Stay alert," I warn.

I watch the woods and listen. All I hear is the faint rustling of leaves high up in the trees. I look up just in time to see the Wendigo leaping onto one of the Hounds. It savages him with it's claws and carries him off into the woods. A hail of automatic fire follows it.

This is not getting us anywhere. The Wendigo will just come back and pick us off one by one. Our guns are totally useless. I look over at Agent Johansson and she nods to me almost as if she knows what I'm thinking.

"Shoulder your guns and arm yourselves with Blasters. You in the SUV, put on the flamethrower. We are coming to you," Agent Johansson orders.

I get my Blaster out. It is a small handheld flamethrower. I figure this thing will give the Wendigo something to really scream about when I blast him. The only problem with them is they are only good to a range of about six feet. When the Wendigo is that near, it may already be too late to light his ass on fire.

I move us slowly to the SUV. The Hound inside gets out with a full sized flamethrower strapped to his back. He ignites it and the tip hums as it burns. That thing would put some serious hurt on anything.

The Wendigo howls like the wind off in the distance. "He is probably done with his meal and heading back to us," I say, looking out into the woods but making sure to watch the trees this time.

Scott shoots me a stern look and I figure he is pissed about me calling his man a meal for the Wendigo. This is a bad situation and unless we start doing some serious damage to that thing, we'll all end up in its gut.

"Get into a circle so we can protect our backs," Scott orders.

Everyone rearranges their position so we form a circle. We make use of natural cover and the SUV where we can.

Agent Johansson takes out her SAT phone, presses a key and starts talking. "I want a chopper posted 15 klicks from my position. Primary mission assault, secondary evac," Agent Johansson listens for a moment then hangs up the phone. "They will be on post in thirty minutes."

I don't think we have thirty minutes but I figure speaking my mind would not be helpful. I smell death and decay in the air. "It's back," I whisper into my mic.

It bursts upon us with incredible speed. It claws Scott, runs through the middle of us and grabs one of the Hounds on the other side of our circle. The Hound with the flamethrower lets out a spout of fire that almost hits Agent Johansson and swaths the area just behind the Wendigo's path. He manages to hit the Wendigo and the Hound it's carrying right as they are going out of range. The Wendigo and the Hound scream as the liquid fire burns into them. Their screams continue off in the darkness for a few moments then silence returns. I've had enough and run off into the darkness after the Wendigo. Once I clear the immediate area, I really put on the speed to catch up.

"Logan, come back," Agent Johansson's orders into my ear. Not this time, lady.

I ignore her and keep hunting the Wendigo. I made the mask and came here to kill this thing so I could set Caleb's spirit free. That is what I intend to do.

A wolf howls off in the distance, which I think is strange since it's the first animal I've ever heard when the Wendigo is around.

I chase the beast several klicks in a very short time. We are both moving at a very fast run, leaping across any obstacles that get in our way. I'm pushing the abilities I got from the mask of the Wendigo. I know I'm moving faster than a fleeing deer could even go. I've the scent of the Wendigo and even spot a glimpse of it here and there. It's still carrying the Hound and must know it is being hunted because it should have stopped by now.

A wolf's howl comes from much closer. The Wendigo drops the Hound it's carrying and keeps going. I bend over the body and check him for vitals. He is still alive but unconscious. He is badly burned and clawed. I really want to catch the Wendigo but if I don't get this man some medical attention, he will die.

In the moment I take to consider going back with the wounded Hound or continuing on, I'm attacked. A giant wolf slams into me knocking me into a nearby tree. The wind leaves my lungs and I gasp for air. The wolf stands between me and the Hound bearing its fangs. It's bigger than any wolf I have ever seen, easily twice the size of even a large wolf. It's the jet black of night and has eyes that look more like a mans, than a wolf's eyes. "Easy boy. I just want to help my friend," I say in a calming steady voice.

The wolf almost seems startled by my words. It smells the air and walks around me sniffing. Then all at once, it turns into a man. He is dressed in

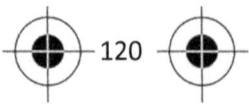

traditional Indian buckskins and is powerfully built. He stands almost 6′ tall and has short jet-black hair. He looks to be of Native American descent. "What are you doing here?" He demands.

"I'm...um...hunting the Wendigo. It carried my friend off," I stammer, still shocked by the fact he was a wolf just a moment ago.

"What do you know of the flesh eater?" He asks.

"It was once my cousin, Caleb. I have sworn to kill the Wendigo he has become, to free his spirit."

"The flesheater is a blight on our land. I will kill it if I catch it. You should leave this place for it is protected," he says, sweeping his arm all around.

Then he shape changes into a ten-foot tall werewolf and howls at the moon, which is not quite full yet. He glances back at me, drops to all fours and bounds off in the direction the Wendigo was going.

"What is going on Logan? Who were you talking to?" comes Agent Johansson's voice in my ear.

I pick up the Hound and head back to the SUV much slower than I came since I'm carrying my injured comrade and don't want to hurt him anymore than he already is. "I'm not sure you would believe me if I told you. I found the wounded Hound and am coming back," I respond to Agent Johansson as I walk.

"What about the Wendigo?" Agent Johansson asks.

"He has bigger problems than us at the moment," I smile, almost laughing to myself. I feel a little punch drunk from the excitement of the evening.

By the time I get back, the chopper is almost here. Scott works on the wounded man to get him stable while Agent Johansson takes me to the side. "I want to know what happened out there."

"Um...well, a werewolf came across my path. He was hunting the Wendigo," I finally just blurt out.

"How do you know it was a werewolf?"

"It was first in giant wolf form, then that of a man and then that of a ten foot tall man-wolf. I figure that is a werewolf," I say, getting kind of annoyed.

Agent Johansson thinks for a moment and drops the conversation. She does not seem rattled at all that I just had an encounter with a werewolf. I wonder if this is just another average day to her? If so, this job is really interesting. Guess there are no water cooler chats here.

We bug out on the chopper. The uninjured Hound takes the SUV. In the chopper, Agent Johansson talks to me.

"I want you to come to my home base for some more training. Would you be up for that?" Agent Johansson asks.

"Sure. I don't think we'll have much luck hunting the Wendigo as long as that werewolf is on it's trail."

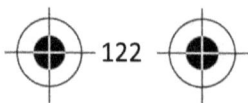

"The thing is my people are very sensitive about who they let into our facility. It would help if I could tell them you were joining our organization."

"I'm not sure I am ready for that. This is personal for me. Caleb was my friend and cousin. I will work with you as long as he is trapped in the Wendigo and you are helpful."

"Some of our researchers feel there might be a way to change Caleb back to his human self. Those are the kind of things our organization can offer you," Agent Johansson tempts me.

"I would be very interested in learning more about changing Caleb back. Is my price for the information joining your organization?"

"No, but we could use a good man like you. There are few men in the world who could track a Wendigo at night without even night vision equipment," Agent Johansson admits, but I know she is just too damn smart. She knows I can see in the dark. I can see it in her eyes. I always feel like I'm the prey when dealing with Agent Johansson and she is the master hunter putting traps down right where I am going to step.

"I will admit I share a connection to the Wendigo but that will not help me with other monsters."

"I am willing to take that chance. Join us and you will be able to truly make a difference in this world,"

Agent Johansson says, looking me in the eye with a determined look on her face.

I look at her a little skeptically as I ask. "How do you make a difference? What does your organization do?"

"We do a lot of watching and researching of all aspects of the supernatural. I personally work mainly with capture and destruction of ones that become a danger to Norms or normal people." Agent Johansson pauses then continues. "We are charged with monitoring and protecting humanity from supernatural creatures. We are a secret organization from Norms and supernaturals alike. We use the powers of existing organizations around the world to cut through the red tape as needed." She sounds a little like a car salesman, trying to convince me to take a test drive.

"Would I be able to have a normal life? Have a family, a wife and kids?"

"Our lives are not normal. We work case by case so we can have a lot of time off only to be called away in the middle of the night. Keeping a family is very difficult," Agent Johansson confesses as I notice her playing with the engagement ring on the wrong hand. Now more than ever I feel she probably lost a relationship that was very dear to her. I don't know if I'm ready to do that, I want to be a father and husband someday.

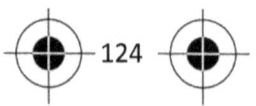

"If I was guaranteed that I could have enough time away to have a normal life then, yes I would join." The idea intrigues me but I am not able to give up my whole life.

"We can give you the right to refuse most cases. From time to time, there will be one that requires your specific abilities. Those cases you would need to take."

"But I could refuse other cases, right? If that is agreed to and I'm promised enough time to have a real family life, I will give it a shot," I agree, taking a moment to look at the vast lonely forest below.

"This is not something you just give a shot. If you join up, you are in for life. You may move to inactive status and just be an advisor but you can never just walk away. The things you learn and experience in this job are far beyond government top-secret rating. Joining us is a commitment to a way of life. It says that you believe in protecting the rest of mankind from things that go bump in the night. We are the first and often also the last line of defense Norms have. Thankfully most supernaturals live secretive lives and don't harm people. But some get out of hand and have to be dealt with either by other supernaturals or us."

The tree tops sweep by under the chopper as I think. The Wendigo will be hard for me to find and defeat on my own, but I have to do this on my own terms. "I agree with what you are doing but I'm not willing to lose my freedom to it. I think for now I will go my own way. I will work with you, but not for you." I decide for now this is the best course of action.

"Very well. In that case, we cannot go to our main base. We will divert to another facility," Agent Johansson says, typing away at her phone to make the necessary arrangements.

About an hour later, which is early morning, we land at a complex way out in the middle of nowhere. It's made up of one large building and two smaller ones. The whole area is surrounded by a security fence. It has a landing strip and four guard towers. It looks like a military facility. I know we are still in Canada.

We get some food and are assigned rooms in one of the smaller buildings. My room is small like a dorm room. There is a bed, desk, chair, dresser and a closet. No window, TV, computer or bathroom. Even so, I'm glad to get some rest. I lay down and soon fall asleep.

****

A knocking on my door wakes me. "Yes," I mutter, rubbing my eyes.

"Time to start training, Logan. There are fatigues in the dresser you can wear. You have time for a quick shower if you want. It's at the end of the hall. Be out front in thirty," Scott says through my door.

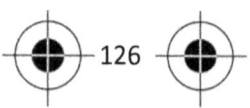

I take a shower and get dressed in the military issue fatigues. Out front, Scott and a couple other men are waiting for me. One of them is the uninjured Hound from last night. From the look of the sun, it's midafternoon. I could have used more rest but then I probably wouldn't have slept tonight.

Scott waves me over and we all jog around the base once then go over to a firing range. They run me through the paces with a couple of different automatic weapons including machine guns. I shoot pretty well but it's good to become more familiar with the weapons. I have never used a full auto burst before and have trouble keeping on my target at first. My shots keep wanting to climb up to the right, especially with longer bursts.

Next, we practice with Blasters. The mini flamethrowers take some getting used to. They are unlike anything I've ever used before. We practice with them for the rest of the afternoon. Right before dinner, I get to try out a full size flamethrower. It is awesome in its power. I'm in awe and afraid of it at the same time. It's not a weapon I would want to use unless I had to. I saw what it did to the Hound that was hit with it. The men say it's on the banned weapon list for most militaries of the world because of its horrific power. Governments have mustered the courage to ban this weapon but we have no problem using it against something we consider outside humanity. What does that say about us?

After training, we go to dinner and bed. I'm tired and looking forward to getting a good nights rest.

Chapter 12: Dreamcatcher

I'm creeping down the dark hallways of the facility. With head raised, I smell the air. The scents of several humans can be identified but one stands out. Her smell is sweet and calls to me.

PAIN surges through my gut. I'm so hungry. Her sweet meat will fill me up. I move through the halls hunting her by scent. The pain comes in waves, surging through me. I need to feast on her subtle flesh. I need to eat now.

I stop in front of a door and sniff. Her scent excites me as it fills my head. She is just beyond this door. I must have her. The door handle does not turn. Rage fills me as I'm so close to the one that will fulfill my desire. I pit my strength against the doors. It whines as the metal bends to my will. The door slowly swings open.

There before me is my prize. How juicy her naked body looks. I must taste her succulent flesh. The scent of her sweet skin calls to me. I sneak to the side of her bed. The "thump, thump, thump" of her heart calls to me like a dinner bell. A wave of hunger PAIN, doubles me over.

"What the hell are you doing, Logan," I hear Agent Johansson's voice say.

I spiral in darkness heading toward a light. Then all at once, I'm myself and no longer the Wendigo. I look up to see a very surprised Agent Johansson in her bed looking at me. She appears to be naked with the sheet pulled up around her. I know this image will fill my mind with all sorts of fantasies later when I have time to recall it.

I'm confused and it must show on my face. Agent Johansson studies me as I stand erect and try to figure out what just happened. I think the Wendigo took over my body and I saw it as a dream.

"I'm sorry. I must have been sleepwalking," I offer as an explanation, starting to pick up the mangled door and wedging it back in place.

"So your dreams are about me?" Agent Johansson questions with a slight smile.

"Yeah. They sure were tonight," I admit, feeling a little embarrassed but also very aroused at the sight of her in bed with her hair down.

"Next time just knock," Agent Johansson suggests.

I stand there not knowing what to do. Agent Johansson is looking me over so I look down. I'm naked except for my underwear. I guess when the Wendigo took me over he forgot to put on my pants before going off to eat people. This thought makes me

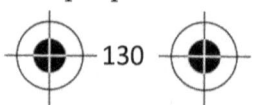

smile and Agent Johansson sees my smile and thinks it's meant for her. She scoots over and lifts the edge of her sheet inviting me in.

I don't think at all. I just climb in. My wildest fantasies couldn't compete with the reality of being with Agent Johansson.

In the morning, when I wake, Agent Johansson is gone and clothes are laid out on a chair for me. I get dressed and go find Scott.

"I need to spend the day working on a protective talisman," I say, not sure how to explain.

"You are scheduled to train with me today. Why don't you run it by Agent Johansson?" He suggests, looking a little annoyed.

"Where is she?" I ask, looking around for her.

"Over in the main building," he says, pointing.

I walk over and find Agent Johansson in an office going over some files. I can't help but smile at her as the memories of last night flood my mind. She looks up at me and seems to be all business. I wonder if last night was a one-time thing or will we be continuing tonight?

"I would like to go into the woods today to make a talisman to use against the Wendigo."

"Is this necessary?" Agent Johansson asks, stacking paperwork and folding her arms over her chest before looking up.

"Yes, I think it is."

"Then do what you need to do," she says, looking back down at the files before her.

It's like we were never together. She is back to her cool calm demeanor. I don't claim to understand women enough to know what that means. Maybe it is a work thing for her.

I get a member of the staff to show me where I can find some yarn. I end up having to settle for a thin cord. I go by my room and get into my bag. I take out the mask of the Wendigo and cut a small lock of hair off. I get some tobacco in a pouch and a lighter. With all my supplies, I head into the woods.

Once way out of sight of the facility I start running fast. I'm looking for a willow tree. I know I'm pretty far north to find one. Luckily, this facility is in southern Canada. It takes me three hours of running through the woods to find a suitable willow tree. I cut a length about eight inches long of a supple branch. I sit down and slowly bend the branch into a teardrop shape. I take the cord, tie the branch together and then wrap the cord all the way around the branch. I continue to wrap the branch with one continuous piece of cord until all the wood is covered. Next, I cross the teardrops shape eight times with the cord to represent the eight legs of a spider. Then I go around the eight strands that run through the middle of the frame in a spiral pattern making a spider's web. When it's complete, I tie the lock of the Wendigo's hair onto

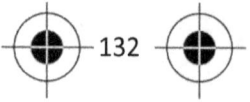

it in the middle of the web. I burn some of the tobacco and blow it over the dreamcatcher I've made. The smoke cleanses the dreamcatcher and awakens it. I tie the remaining bag of tobacco into the dreamcatcher. I also make a smaller version of the dreamcatcher to wear as a necklace.

I return to base as the sun is setting. I'm starving but go to my room first. I tie the large dreamcatcher at the head of my bed. The other one I intend to wear on me all the time as a necklace. My hope is the dreamcatcher will protect me from ever being taken over by the Wendigo again. They are supposed to capture evil dreams and let good ones through. Every day I will need to hang the dreamcatchers in the rays of the sun so the bad things caught in them can be destroyed by the sunlight.

Dreamcatchers are not a traditional custom of my tribe but I learned about them in college. If the legends of the Wendigo are true then it seems to me that other legends can also be true. It also just felt right for me to make the dreamcatchers. That to me is enough of a reason to make them. I had to do something to protect my mind from the Wendigo. Next time it takes me over, I might kill someone.

I go to the mess hall to get dinner then return to my room to get some sleep. I consider going to Agent Johansson's door and knocking this time. I'm not sure that is the right move. It's hard for me to envision a lasting relationship with her. But what's wrong with just sex. I'm so confused about it. The thought of Agent Johansson naked in her bed boils my blood enough to make the decision for me. I get up, put on clothes and head to Agent Johansson's room.

I notice that the door has been replaced since I broke the old one the night before. This fact holds my hand for a moment but my blood is still on fire for Agent Johansson so I knock. A couple moments later Agent Johansson opens the door. She is in a skin tight t-shirt that just comes down to the bottom of her ass. I don't think she has anything on underneath. She watches me ogle her body, waiting for me to make the first move.

I lean down to kiss her but she pulls back. "Can I come in?" I ask, sounding a little more desperate than I like.

"Sure. If you can tell me about how you broke my door last night?" Agent Johansson says, eyeing me up and down.

"Um...I was sleepwalking."

"I think that might be true but how did you break my door?"

"I'm pretty strong," I say, striking a pose and flexing for her, trying to lighten the issue.

Agent Johansson grins slightly. "Yes, but it would have taken incredible strength to do that and not wake me."

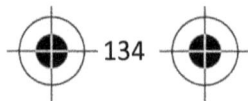

"What do you want me to say? I really wanted to be in here with you," I say smiling.

"If you want me so bad, you can do it again. As an incentive, if you can get in, you can stay in," Agent Johansson whispers seductively as she shuts and locks the door.

I'm too hot and bothered to think it over. I just grab the door handle and rip it off. I push in the door and shut it behind me. Agent Johansson is very surprised, but pleased. As I see the smile fill her face, I wonder if it's for me or for what she just confirmed I can do. Our lips meet and I don't worry about such things anymore.

Chapter 13:
It's Here

I can smell him now. Soon I will feast of his flesh. The hunger pains surges through my gut. I lean my head back to let out the howling wind raging inside of me. Hurriedly I follow the scent of my prey through the woods.

I come to a massive rock with bits of wood shavings and cord all around. His smell is strong here. He must have sat here for a while. His smell fills my nose and his trail is renewed by the strength of the scent. Quickly I bound through the forest following the scent trail.

Up ahead there is light. Metal structures and light where there should be only darkness. My prey is in there. The new smells of this place fill me. There are many prey here. I can feast for days on their succulent meat.

One of my prey is close. I track it walking just inside a great metal fence. I come from behind and leap the fence in a single bound. I pounce upon my prey and devour him. Blood and flesh splatter as I frantically try to sate my hunger.

Moments later my hunger has subsided enough to move on. I will come back and eat the rest later. Now I must hunt the Longstride. He is my enemy. I will enjoy devouring his power along with his flesh.

I dash across the open ground to a metal building. I follow the scent trail into the building. Each door I pass brings flesh smells of manthings for me to eat. I have to fight to keep focused on finding Longstride. After I've feasted on his flesh and blood, the others will fall easily before me.

A door opens. A dark haired woman looks into my eyes. Horror flashes across her eyes as my claw rips most of her neck out. I lap at her warm blood. My teeth tear at her soft flesh enjoying the feel of each chunk of her flesh passing down my throat. She twitches as I feed, taking the last of her life into me. Her flesh feeds my hunger.

Once sated, I move on down the hall. Longstrides's scent is strong here. I smell all around the door and know this is the den of my prey. I push upon the door…

****

I leap out of bed butt naked with Enuk's knife in my hand. The Wendigo is outside my door and I'm going to meet it in battle.

"What are you doing, Logan?" says a very sleepy Agent Johansson.

What am I doing? It should be in the room by now. I open the door, still naked and look up and down the hall. There is no body of a dark haired girl and certainly no Wendigo.

"Logan?" Agent Johansson questions.

Then it hits me. The Wendigo was outside my room. I'm in Agent Johansson's room. "The Wendigo is inside the compound. It's inside my room. Sound the alarm," I say pulling on my pants and shoes. I don't bother with a shirt, there is no time. I set out to hunt the Wendigo as Agent Johansson alerts the Hounds.

I run with Enuk's knife in my hand down the halls. I turn a corner and there is the naked blood soaked form of Caleb. He shows his teeth, straightens his clawed fingers and barrels down the hallway at me. I charge at him and we meet in a bloody crash. We are whirling devils each needing to kill the other. I drive Enuk's knife deep into the Wendigo's flesh over and over, as I try to dodge its deadly claws. I'm slashed across the chest and my left forearm. Pain rings through me but I'm too focused on my oath to free Caleb's spirit to let anything stop me. Even if I must trade my life for the Wendigo's death, I will do it.

I know we are moving faster than any human can. We are a blur of slashing blade and claws. Enuk's knife catches the Wendigo in the shoulder, rendering

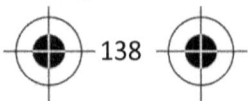

its right arm useless at least for now. It screams in pain, "WaaaEee!"

The Wendigo whirls around and manages to bite into my left shoulder. My left hand catches its left claw as it comes down. With the Wendigo still biting into my shoulder, I stab it in the neck with Enuk's knife. It tries to scream but only blood gurgles up its throat. It locks eyes with me and stops struggling. The dead yellow eyes of the Wendigo change to the light brown of Caleb's eyes. I see the friend and cousin I knew in those eyes. They call out to me for help.

"Pop, pop, pop," sounds of machine gun fire coming from down the hall, riddling the Wendigo. Its eyes flash to yellow as it rips itself free of me. It bounds down the hall, through the Hound that was shooting at it and out of the building.

I slump on the floor and see Agent Johansson standing in the hallway the opposite way the Wendigo went. She has an almost evil grin on her face. I wonder how long she has been there. She could have seen it all, which means she knows I have beyond human abilities. This could get ugly.

Agent Johansson calls for medical assistance and comes over to me. She rips off the bottom half of her shirt and uses it to help stop the bleeding. The medics arrive soon and I'm taken away to the infirmary.

The next day I'm feeling good and ready to get back to work. The doctor freaks when I get out of bed. He comes over and looks at my wounds but they are all healed up. He is so shocked he can't even speak, so I just walk out. I head back to my room to think.

Chapter 14:
Powers Reveled

Caleb is still inside the Wendigo. I saw his eyes and I know he knows me. If there is a way to save Caleb from the Wendigo curse, I have to try it. He would do the same for me. My thoughts are interrupted by a knock at the door.

I put my hand on Enuk's knife and call, "Come in."

Agent Johansson swings the door open. "Let's go for a walk, Logan."

I pull on my boots and follow Agent Johansson down the hall. We head out into the yard and through the main gate. We walk about a mile into the woods before Agent Johansson starts talking. "You are doing amazingly well, considering the fight you had just a few hours ago."

"I'm a fast healer," I say, breathing in the crisp clean air scented with pine.

"You didn't used to be a fast healer. You were in the hospital for well over a week with your shoulder wound up in Alaska. What changed?"

"I don't really want to answer these kind of questions," I try to distract Agent Johansson by walking away but she is too focused on her goal to get the information she wants.

"You have exhibited powers of the supernatural. So you must be straight with me or we'll have an issue. You know my organization polices the supernaturals of the world. Some of them even work with us. But you need to be honest with me so I can help you."

"Why are we out here in the woods and not in your office?" I ask, somewhat impatiently. I want this conversation to be over.

"Because I am the only one who truly knows some of the things you can do. Sure the doctor thinks you can heal way too fast but he can be silenced. I want you, Logan, to tell me what is going on so I can decide what to do with the knowledge I have."

"I could just kill you and leave with my secret safe," I say, but I know there is little conviction in my voice.

"The Logan I know could never do that. Anyway, my organization would definitely hunt you down then."

"It seems I've little choice," I say with a resigned sigh. I turn away from Agent Johansson and start off into the forest.

"I'm sorry, Logan, but this is my job, my life's work. If you are straight with me I can help you."

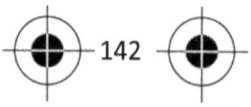

"After my fight with the Wendigo in Alaska, I had a vision from an Indian spirit. The spirit told me how to gain powers of the Wendigo so I could hunt it. Once back home, I performed the ritual and gained the powers you have witnessed."

"How did you know the Wendigo was in your room last night?"

"I have a connection to the Wendigo. When I sleep I can sometimes see what it sees."

"Can it see through your eyes?"

"I think it could before I made the dreamcatchers," I admit, holding up the dreamcatcher necklace I'm wearing to show her.

"So this little thing protects you but still allows you to see through its eyes?" Agent Johansson questions skeptically, examining the dreamcatcher as much as she can without touching it.

"Yes, I can feel it working." I tuck the necklace back into my shirt.

"Do many Indians have magical powers?"

"I'm the only one that I know of."

"You do not seem like a threat to Norms. I will keep your secret for now," Agent Johansson promises, giving me her hand to seal the bargain we have made.

"Thank you," I reply, formally, shaking her hand.

"Where do we go from here? Do you have a plan of how to kill the Wendigo?" she asks, walking leisurely back toward camp.

"It's actively hunting me and will come back sooner or later, so we need to be better prepared." I say, pausing for a moment to think. "I want to see the information you have about removing the curse of the Wendigo from Caleb. Last night, for just a moment, Caleb was in control of the Wendigo. His spirit is trapped inside that cursed beast. If there is a way to save him, I have to try."

"Ok, Logan, I will get what information I can."

After dinner, Agent Johansson delivers the data she has on exorcizing the Wendigo's corrupting spirit out of a person. I spend most of the night reading through all of it. I can tell that the information is incomplete. It speaks of many of the components of the ritual but doesn't explain how it's performed. It gives me a place to start, but is not the solution I was looking for.

I know in my heart that I have already decided on a course of action. I want to try to capture the Wendigo in hopes that I can one day find a way to free Caleb from it. Capturing the Wendigo will not be an easy task. I will have to come up with a good plan and have Agent Johansson's full cooperation to succeed.

The next day I go to Agent Johansson to talk. "The research on lifting the curse of the Wendigo is incomplete but there is enough there to give me hope

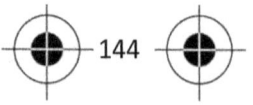 144

that a cure could be found. So I want to try to catch and contain the Wendigo."

"Really? How do you propose we do that?" Agent Johansson lifts her eyebrow.

"I'm not totally sure. We would have to lure it somewhere enclosed, impossible to break out of. Your organization hunts monsters. Don't you have super tasers or tranq darts or something?"

"Yes. We have several weapon systems we could try, and we have high security holding facilities that could contain the Wendigo if we can capture it in one."

"Are you willing to help me trap and hold the Wendigo?"

"We have taken several casualties trying to kill the Wendigo. Capturing it will most likely be even more treacherous. Then you want us to hold the Wendigo until a cure can be found. You probably even want me to involve our research department on working to find the rest of your cure. Am I right?"

"Yeah, that should do it," I grin.

"I could sell this idea better if you joined our organization," Agent Johansson informs, a little frustration leaking into her voice. I know then how badly she wants me to join. But I'm also realizing the cost of such a decision.

"So if I sign up, you will help. If not, we stick to killing it?"

"I cannot say for certain, but yes, that is the most likely outcome."

I'm willing to give my life just to kill the Wendigo so why am I so hesitant to join this organization to possibly save Caleb from his curse. My grandfather told me that he thinks I've been chosen to be a hunter and to live and die by the knife. I guess if I accept Agent Johansson's offer I'm heading further down that path and that scares me. I'm not afraid of dying or pain, but I dread the loss of living a life of peace. Am I truly destined to hunt and be hunted all my life? Is that all I can expect from my future? In the past, the hunters of my tribe were respected and lived well. They protected and provided for the people. They had wives and families. Who am I to say that is not a good life? I will take up the knife of the hunter and protect the people. But one day I will also have the family that I will have earned. The men in my family have said this is my path and I need to accept it and quit fighting my fate.

"I will join if you give me the ability to choose my missions, so I can have enough down time to have a normal life and you agree to help me capture and contain the Wendigo indefinitely."

"I am sure your terms will be accepted. Welcome to the family, Logan," Agent Johansson says, looking a little smug, like the cat who caught the canary.

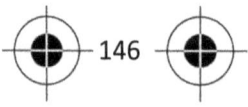

I feel like she has gotten the better of me somehow but I'm not quite sure how. It doesn't really matter, as this seems to be what I'm destined to do. I have made my choice and intend to make the best of it.

The next couple of days are spent formulating a plan to capture the Wendigo. I occasionally smell its deathly odor near the edge of the facility. I will be the bait to lure the Wendigo into our trap.

We create an opening in our defenses around one of the smaller buildings. I walk all around the area even going a short way into the woods and back to the building. I want the Wendigo to have a strong scent trail to follow.

The small structure has been set up as a temporary containment area for the beast. I will be waiting inside, luring it into the trap. The whole area will be monitored with video and motion sensors. When the Wendigo enters the area, forces will move in to surround and contain it. I'm given a gas mask to use, as the first thing to be triggered is some kind of super knockout gas.

Agent Johansson has had special equipment and men flown in for the operation. Scott is still in charge of the Hounds, but as always, Agent Johansson is in overall command. Scott arranges his Hounds into six four-man teams. Two teams will operate turret mounted super tazers on the back of jeeps. These babies have enough juice to drop elephants with one shot. One team is allocated to tranquilizer sniper duty. They will be using a special cocktail designed to put supernaturals to sleep. From my understanding after the little time I've trained with these guys, the tranqs often do not work. Each supernatural type has different resistances and they rarely get the chance to test tranq darts. So these best guess concoctions may drop the Wendigo or just piss it off. Two other teams are armed with taser rifles. These things pack ten times the kick of the traditional hand held variety. The last team is armed with Blasters and flamethrowers. They are the "holy-shit let's just kill the damn thing" option. All teams have at least one Blaster and standard weapons issued to them.

We set the trap and I wait in the building as bait. I'm armed with Enuk's knife, a combat knife, a blaster and a taser rifle. Hours pass and no sign of the Wendigo. A cot is brought in and we give the team's a rotation so they can get some rest. Dawn comes and still no sign of the Wendigo. Everyone is tired and frustrated but we keep to the plan.

I get some sleep as the day wears on. Midafternoon I'm awakened by a voice in my ear mic. "Contact at north perimeter fence."

I get up and get ready. My primary goal will be to hit the Wendigo with the taser rifle as it closes on

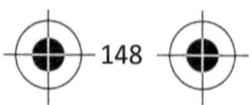

me. "Contact heading towards Logan," one of the Hound's reports.

"Everyone give the creature room. No one move in until I give the signal," Scott's voice commands over my ear mic.

I know this was my strategy, but I have to fight fear from rising up inside me. My intention was to be trapped inside this area with the Wendigo. I'm not foolish enough to believe I will escape unscathed. I slip my gas mask half on, ready to pull it over my face and raise my taser rifle in preparation of the coming battle.

"Contact is entering the trap through the north door," a Hound reports.

I smell the Wendigo before I see it. The stench of death fills my head as a premonition of what lies ahead for one of us. It moves into sight and I follow it in the sights of my rifle. It moves into the clear. I let out my breath and squeeze the trigger. Four barbs attached to ultra-thin wires spiral out and eat into the Wendigo's flesh. "WaaaEee!" the Wendigo screams as thousands of volts surge through its body. It thrashes around until it sees me. Its eyes fill with rage at the sight of me and it charges. I hold down the trigger on the taser rifle sending electricity into its body continuously. It staggers but keeps on coming.

"KABOOM!" The building rumbles as all the gas canisters are set off.

I pull the gas mask over my face. As the wave of gas washes over us, the Wendigo attacks. I drop my rifle and pull Enuk's knife in my right hand and a military style combat knife in the other hand. The Wendigo's charge knocks me off balance and we both tumble to the floor. I'm up an instant later scanning all around for my opponent. The gas is so thick I can't see anything, especially through my gas mask. I'm constantly spinning around trying to catch sight of the Wendigo.

Pain surges through my back as the Wendigo claws me. I twirl around just in time to parry its next attack with my combat knife. I sweep Enuk's knife across its chest, cutting a deep gash. Savagely, the Wendigo flails into me with both clawed arms. I'm pushed back, by the constant attack.

"Is the gas affecting the target?" Scott asks.

"Not even a little, and I can't see a damn thing!"

"Vent gas and all teams move in," Scott orders.

I don't have time to think about Scott and the Hounds. The Wendigo is coming after me and soon I slam my back into the wall. This catches me off guard and the Wendigo connects to my left forearm with its claw. Pain surges through my arm but I fight my way through it to keep up my defense. I know the Hounds are coming and I just have to hold out a little longer. The gas is being blown out by huge fans and my vision improves.

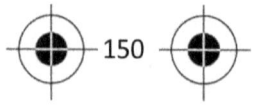

I move along the wall knowing that soon I will have to come to a corner and then I will really be trapped. The Wendigo keeps pressing its attack and I'm forced to constantly dodge and parry. It's moving so damn fast that it is hard for me to keep up. I want to remove my gas mask as the gas is mostly clear but I can't afford the time.

"The gas is cleared. Everyone move in," Scott orders, over my ear mic.

That news gives me a second wind. They are coming. Just a little bit longer and I will have help. I can do that. I know I can. The Wendigo keeps thrashing at me with its deadly claws. I can feel my blood flowing out of the wound on my back and arm. I'm weakening from the loss of blood, but I have to keep going to stay alive.

When I think I cannot hold on any longer, I see a jeep drive into the building. I force myself not to look at it and focus on the Wendigo. I parry and dodge blow after blow. My shoulder hits a wall and I know I've come to the corner. The Wendigo's eyes dance with a demonic joy as it knows it has me. I parry all the incoming blows I can but some get through to savage my flesh.

Pain washes over me but it's different from before. My body jerks violently and I know I've been hit by the jeep mounted super tasers. Thankfully, the Wendigo took most of the jolt and I only got a small percentage of the assault. Even that is almost enough to drive me toward unconsciousness. I struggle to stay on my feet. All I can do is lean against the wall for support and watch the battle unfold.

The Wendigo turns on the jeep and makes the forty-foot leap on one bound. It mutilates the Hounds in the jeep and runs towards the other teams heading for it. It's hit by multiple tranq darts but just keeps going. The area is filled with taser wire. Some that hits its mark and others that fly wild. The Wendigo leaps across the floor and heads for the locked door. It hits the door with all it's might but is trapped. We planned for this but thought we could bring it down. Now I'm not sure we can.

The Wendigo turns and lets out its howling wail before charging back into the fray. The Hound teams are resorting to using blasters and flamethrowers. Small fires are started all over and the building begins to fill with smoke. The Wendigo is hit and screams. "WaaaEeee!"

I can tell the Wendigo is only interested in flight at this point. It leaps up to the rafters and rips its way into the air ducts. I watch as it quickly moves through the ducts and out of the building.

I slump to the floor and finally allow myself to relax. I close my eyes and no longer fight to stay awake. Soon I'm in the comforting arms of darkness.

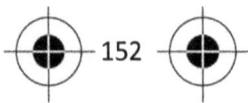

Chapter 15:
The Scarred One

The next day, I wake in the infirmary, almost completely healed. I make my way to Agent Johansson's office. She is working away behind her desk as normal. I go in and slump down in a chair, still a little aware of my wounds.

"We lost three men and five others were wounded. Unless we come up with a hell of a good plan we are just going to have to kill that thing. I cannot afford to keep losing so many men." Agent Johansson states, looking up at me.

I feel wretched. My plan didn't work and led to the death of good men. That damn Wendigo is just too hard to take down. I held back in the fight because I wanted to save Caleb, not kill him. Now any hope of getting Caleb back might be lost. There must a way to capture the thing. I'm not willing to give up yet.

"I need some time to think," I tell Agent Johansson, rubbing my face with my hands. "I'm exhausted by this damn monster."

"I understand, Logan, but if it starts killing again, I will have to do something." She looks at me sympathetically, but I know she can't back down with lives at stake

"I understand," I say, getting up to leave.

I walk the facility grounds and feel lost. I feel alone and not connected to the people here. I need my family. I need the wisdom of my fathers and the comfort of Jessy. I call home, hoping I can get some grounding back in my life.

"Hello," comes the familiar voice of my father through the phone.

"Hey dad, how's everything going?" I ask, but I can hear and feel the stress in my voice. It is a relief to hear his voice.

"We are all the same. Amos did find an Iroquois up in Canada who survived an attack by the creature you hunt. Amos has gone to meet with him to see what he knows."

"I would like to meet this survivor as well. Where are they meeting?"

"I'm not sure? Call your grandfather and get the details from him. I understand it is quite a journey into the woods."

"How's Faith doing?"

"She is ever the shining star. She looks more and more like your mother all the time." Even as my father says this, I can hear the sorrow in his voice. He has never given up on my mother and loves her still.

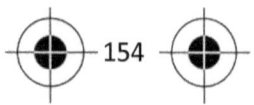

"Have you heard from Jessy?" I ask, trying to change the subject.

"She has called and stopped by a couple times. She misses you as we all do. How has your hunting trip been?" My father asks, probably thinking it's not a good idea to talk about the Wendigo openly.

"I've not been able to bring down my prey, but have had it in my sights a few times. It's more powerful and cunning than I thought. There is hope of capturing it and curing it of it's illness."

"I didn't know there was a cure. I wish you luck on your hunt, my son."

"Tell everyone hi from me. I will continue my hunt. Take care of yourself, father. I will call again when I can," I say, hanging up the phone.

I call Amos and make arrangements to meet him later today. He is only about a two-hour flight away from here by helicopter.

I head over to Agent Johansson's office. "I want to go meet an Iroquois who knows about the Wendigo. My grandfather Amos found him and has arranged a meeting for tomorrow. I will need to get a chopper to take me there," I say, hoping Agent Johansson will go for the idea.

"You think this person might have something useful to tell us?" Agent Johansson asks, not convinced.

"I'm not sure but it's worth a try. I will be back in a day, maybe two."

"Ok we'll go. Be ready to leave in an hour."

"You are coming?" I ask, kind of surprised.

"Is that a problem?"

"I...um...don't think so," I stammer, but thinking it may be. If my grandfather's contacts are extremely traditional they won't want any non-Indians present.

Agent Johansson, four heavily armed Hounds and I head away from the facility in a helicopter an hour later. When we arrive at a small airstrip close to where I'm to meet my grandfather, there is a black SUV waiting for us. I don't know how Agent Johansson does it. She is always planning ahead and prepared for anything. This may be an interesting trip.

We drive to the Moose Rutter, the lodge Amos is staying in for the night. Agent Johansson arranges for rooms for her and the Hounds. I stay in my grandfather's room.

My grandfather, Amos Longstride, is glad to see me. We spend some time catching up and I tell him about my encounters with the Wendigo and the possible ritual to free Caleb of the Wendigo spirit. Amos listens and nods as I tell my tale.

"You have learned much. I hope the one I found can be helpful to you. I have never spoken to the actual survivor of the Wendigo attack but arranged

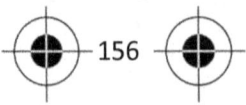

the meeting through his grandson. The survivor of the Wendigo attack is a shaman of the Iroquois and quite revered. We are being honored just to meet him." Amos says, pausing to think a minute. "He lives in the deep woods by the old ways. The ones who care for him are very traditional and I do not think they will allow your white friends to enter their sacred forest. You should prepare them for this outcome," Amos advises me.

"I figured they wouldn't be very welcome. I'll tell them, you and I will have to go alone."

We go to bed and I think about what lies ahead of me. I want to free Caleb of the Wendigo spirit but at what cost. Is Caleb's one life worth the many that have died trying to capture him? It might be to me but I'm not so sure about Agent Johansson and her employer. Hell, I'm not so sure about my own feelings. Caleb is family and there is little I would not pay for his return, but I would not ask the same of others. Men have given their life to try to capture Caleb and we have only failed. How many more men will I allow to die before I decide too many have died? If Caleb were here, he would say too many have already died for him. I'm unhappy with my thoughts and have a fitful night's sleep. My dreams are filled with vague feelings of having lost something and not being able to find it.

The next morning I explain the situation about non Native Americans not being welcome to Agent Johansson. She is not pleased and insists on coming along as far as they will permit.

We drive thirty minutes to a trailhead. There we are met by two young bucks of the Iroquois. They are dressed traditionally in every way even down to their bows as weapons. Their garb is of the pre-white man era. Their knives are obsidian as are their arrow tips.

As an anthropologist, it's amazing to see people living this way. I've been to reenactments but something is always missed in the outfits. It's usually that the clothes are not real animal skins or that they have been sewn on a sewing machine and not by hand. Sometimes it's only they have just used modern thread. But these two Iroquois are perfect.

The two warriors eye Agent Johansson and the well-armed Hounds with suspicion. One of them approaches as the other lingers in the woods.

"What is your name and purpose here?" The warrior asks in perfect Iroquois.

"I am Amos Longstride and this is my grandson Logan Longstride. These others are friends who wish to come with us. We seek counsel with the Scarred One," Amos says in Iroquois.

"You and your grandson may come, but your...friends...must stay," the warrior says, almost spitting out the word friends.

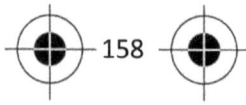

"Only Amos and I will be allowed to go. We'll be back in a few days," I say turning to Agent Johansson.

For just a second, I spot displeasure cross Agent Johansson's face but then her cool exterior is back. She is not used to being told what she is allowed to do. Agent Johansson is used to doing whatever she wants.

"I will leave a team at the Moose Rutter if you need them. See you in a couple days Logan," Agent Johansson say, as she comes up and gives me a hug. This is so unlike Agent Johansson that I take a moment to return her embrace. It's not a particularly loving hug, but a hug in front of her men all the same.

"See ya," is all I manage to get off as Agent Johansson and the Hounds return to their vehicle. The men look shocked that The Ice Queen touched me.

The Iroquois warriors lead us into the woods. My grandfather is in good shape for his age but it's still slow going with, rest periods taken every so often. One of the bucks stays with us at all times as the other scouts ahead and sometimes behind us. They are at home in the woods and totally silent. I watch and study them as we travel.

After we have traveled two hours, we are met by a third Iroquois who is older. He is dressed traditionally but his clothes denote that he is more of a shaman. He does not speak to us. He leads our group now and we split off the main path onto a smaller trail. After a few minutes, we come to a small camp of three wood huts and a longhouse. I have seen wonderful replicas of these before but never ones that have been made to be used daily. The scientist in me is fascinated by everything I'm viewing. It's as if we have stepped back in time. I've never read anything in any of my books about a place like this existing. It's hard to believe it could be kept secret from the world. I wonder why they choose to live this way? What reasons could they have?

As if in answer to my thoughts, the shaman speaks. "Things from the outside world are not permitted where you are going. You must place all your belongings in these baskets and be cleansed in the sweat lodge before we proceed."

He leads us to a sweathouse, takes off his garments, and places them in a basket. When he is totally naked, he enters the sweat lodge. Amos and I do the same before entering the sweathouse. I notice when I take off my clothes that there is a small button stuck under my collar. So that was what Agent Johansson was doing when she hugged me. This must be some kind of tracking device, maybe even a bug.

We all sit in silence letting the steam wash over us. The warriors put hot rocks in a pool of water from time to time to keep the steam going. I can smell the herbs that have been added to the water to help with the cleansing.

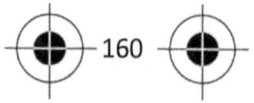

After about thirty minutes, the shaman stands and waves for us to follow him out. We wipe ourselves off with cloths that are provided and dress in traditional buckskins that have been laid out for us. All of our original possessions are nowhere to be seen.

Once we are fully dressed, the shaman speaks to us in Iroquois. "I am called Wolf Watcher. I welcome you among the people. I shall take you to the Scarred One."

We nod in reply. He now sees us as part of the Iroquois people, and worthy of the hospitality of close kin. Before when we were dressed in modern clothing, we were considered outsiders and unclean. By sharing in the cleansing of the sweat lodge and donning their garments, we have become acceptable to them and worthy of knowing his name. These are a very interesting people. I wonder if they all grew up here and have lived their whole life away from the modern world? Surely some of them have seen the outside world.

"In my possessions I have a dreamcatcher necklace and the knife of a dead friend. Is it possible I could have those things?" I ask.

Wolf Watcher considers me for a moment before speaking. "Why do you need these items?"

"I made the dreamcatcher to protect me from being taken over by a Wendigo spirit. I need it especially if I'm going to sleep among the people. The knife is important to me, as it was my friend's knife who was killed by the Wendigo. He charged me with carrying it into battle when I faced the Wendigo before he died."

"You may wear your dreamcatcher and I will bring your friend's knife with me. The fate of the knife will be decided by the Scarred One."

We travel with Wolf Watcher for around five hours through woods and meadows. The two warriors accompany us and I'm aware there are men and wolves shadowing us. I barely see them but with my enhanced senses, I occasionally hear and smell them. We might be considered part of the people, but we are not totally trusted.

I begin to sense cook fires and many people. I know a village is close by but we are not taken near enough to see it. We are led to the base of a mountain, where a small permanent camp has been set up. The camp is made up of two huts and a longhouse. Behind the camp is a great cave leading into the face of the mountain. There are several men in the camp. One of them I recognize as the werewolf I encountered in the woods when I was hunting the Wendigo. I know he remembers me by his stern gaze.

Now I wish I had learned something about werewolves from Agent Johansson. I wonder if all these people are werewolves? That might explain

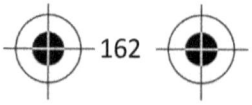

how they remain so hidden from the world. This little trip just became a whole lot more complicated.

As we walk into camp, our every move is watched. Many of the men slowly circle us as if we are their prey and they are sizing us up. I can smell their pheromones that scream aggression and predator. This is an explosive situation. I must be calm and totally non-aggressive.

Amos and I stand in the midst of these warriors. They invade our personal space, touching and smelling us. It's almost like when dogs meet and they walk in circles around one another getting the other's scent and establishing who is dominant. These have to be werewolves.

Soon the strange circling greeting stops and Wolf Watcher leads us into the cave with a couple of the warriors trailing behind. The opening of the cave is huge. I would guess four normal houses could fit inside it's mouth alone. Out of the cave runs a small stream. Our way is lit by torches carried by the warriors. The area is very clean and appears to be lived in during the winter.

The cave passage narrows to twenty feet wide. We follow the stream steadily up into the heart of the mountain. The path we are taking is very well worn. The walls are covered in cave drawings and paintings. This is the picture language of my people. We are not walking quickly but faster than I would like with so much to look at upon the walls. Some of the art appears quite old, but others are recent. I bet they still draw and paint on the walls as their ancestors did. This is a marvelous discovery. There may be more Indian art in this one cave than there is on the rest of the continent combined. The scholar in me wants to start taking pictures and notes, but that would definitely not be welcome here.

We travel through many rooms connected by passageways. Occasionally a passage or room extends off out of sight, so I know there are offshoots and other areas to this massive cave. Some areas have obviously been worked by men to widen or alter the shape. These people have designed this cave to make it their own. The sheer magnitude of the stonework and art speaks of this place being inhabited for many generations.

We walk for at least an hour before pausing to enter a grand cavern that has been unchanged by man. There are huge stalagmites and stalactites in this room. In the far wall is a small waterfall that empties into a large pool that dominates the center of the room. The stream we have been following flows out of this pool. It's a beautiful place. The reflection of our torchlight dance upon the pool and walls giving the whole area a look of little spirits flittering about. I can almost feel the magic in this place.

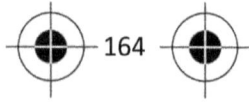

Lying to one side of the pool is an old man. He is dressed as a shaman. He is unmoving and I wonder if he is dead. Wolf Watcher goes up by the old shaman and kneels beside him. He fills a small wooden bowl by dipping it in the pool. He brings the bowl to the old man's lips and slowly pours some of the water in his mouth. I see the old man's mouth fill with water and then slowly drain. Wolf Watcher repeats filling the old shaman's mouth again and again until the bowl is empty.

Wolf Water next takes out a tobacco pipe and lights it. He blows the smoke over the body of the old shaman once in each of the four directions. He then calls forth to the spirits in the language of our people. "Spirit of the Earth Mother I ask you to give us your strength. We come here deep within your breast to awaken the Scarred One. Release him from your comforting embrace so we may gain his wisdom. Please Earth Mother awaken the Scarred One."

The old shaman takes in a breath and then lets it out. I could swear I see dust fly out his nose when he exhales the first time. Could he really have been dead? Did we just witness someone coming back to life? There has to be another explanation. But he was not breathing a moment ago, I'm sure of that. There, I can hear his heart starting to beat. That sound was not evident moments ago. Wow, there is magic in the world that I never thought possible. I feel blessed to have witnessed this resurrection.

The old shaman slowly sits up and I immediately understand why he is called the Scarred One. The right half of his face and neck has been raked by a five-fingered claw, like that of the Wendigo. His right eye is milky white and obviously dead. His left eye is brown, darting around the room, observing everything before it settles upon me.

The Scarred One slowly lifts up his hand and points at me. "You have been touched by the Wendigo. You share it's blood and power. You are the hunter and the hunted. You have compassion for your prey, but it will show none. You seek a cure for your friend, but in doing so you will trap yourself. Ask your questions." The Scarred One says in a deep voice that seems to come from all directions at once.

All eyes are on me as I think of a question. "Can the curse of the Wendigo be lifted?"

"Yes."

"What do I have to do to lift the curse of the Wendigo from Caleb?"

"You must gather the five talons of Raven or the five claws of Coyote. With these, you may call upon the spirit of Raven or Coyote to free Caleb. The spirits will likely demand a payment for their services."

"Where can I find these talons or claws?"

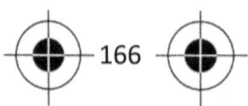

"They are scattered across the land. Each is an item of power in its own right. They will be hidden away or coveted by the greedy. You must find them yourself."

"How will I trap myself by seeking these items to cure Caleb?"

"You already know the answer," the Scarred One says and I figure he is right. By trying to cure Caleb, I will trap myself into living by the knife and becoming part of Agent Johansson's organization.

"How can I trap the Wendigo?"

"The Wendigo is a spirit of the wind. Trying to catch it is like trying to catch the wind. As long as it has power over the wind you will only be able to hold it as if it was air," the Scarred One responds slowly, choosing his words carefully.

"Can I take the power of the wind away from it?" I pray he has a solution to our problem.

"Each element has its opposite. Air has earth. If the Wendigo was within the earth it would become weak."

"I have not been able to knock it unconscious. How can I do this?" I ask, feeling a little hopeful. I never considered trapping it underground.

"The Wendigo never sleeps and cannot be made to rest. It is an ancient spirit that is as restless as the wind. It can be still, calm, steady or a torrent that is almost unstoppable, just like the wind."

I think for a moment, then ask, "Old Broken Nose can redirect wind. Can he help me calm the Wendigo?"

"Old Broken Nose has already given you much. If you want more from him I would ask him yourself."

"How can I speak to Old Broken Nose?"

"He is here watching us. This place is a doorway to the spirit world. I will give him use of my body."

The Scarred One kneels down over the still pool of water and stares into it. I see a silvery form wisp out of the water and flow over and around him. The mist swirls around the Scarred One. Then the wisp flows into the Scarred One through his nose like he was inhaling smoke.

The Scarred One touches his face and looks at his reflection. He then turns to me and his eyes are reflective silver. Even his milky dead eye is a shining silver. I know then that he has been possessed by a spirit. He stands and is unsteady on his feet. He is like a newborn learning to walk again. He soon gains control over his limbs and looks at me.

"Logan, you have done well. I was right to choose you to be a hunter," the spirit of Old Broken Nose says through the Scarred One's mouth. The voice echoes throughout the room much more than when the Scarred One spoke and is more deep and booming.

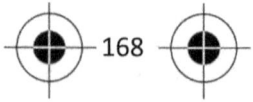

"Thank you, Grandfather Broken Nose. I've tried to use the gifts you have given me well. I want to cure Caleb of the curse of the Wendigo and would like your help," I say, bowing my head out of respect for the ancient spirit.

"I am watching over you, Logan. I have been silent for too long. Many of the people have lost touch with the spirits. This has weakened the spirits. The spirits of science have trapped or confined many of our ancient spirits. For many upon many years, it was all I could do to send simple visions to the False Face Society." Old Broken Nose rests for a minute, seeming to be out of breath. He inhales deeply and a layer of mist from the top of the pool swirls up and into the nose of the Scarred One. He then continues. "When the Wendigo broke through to the world of the people I followed. Caleb and you were to be chosen to join the False Face Society by me so I was watching you. I watched what Caleb became and witnessed you fight him. Then you entered a state of death and I could connect to your spirit. This allowed me to show you the vision and instruct you to make your mask of the Wendigo. When you donned your competed mask, I gained enough power to affect the world again. You have brought me back to the people. For this I thank you," Old Broken Nose says as he inhales more mist from the pool to renew himself.

"I'm honored I could help. The people are better off with your protection," I say, feeling rather overwhelmed that I've been the instrument through which one of our most powerful spirits has been reborn.

"I am still weak but I am no longer trapped. Through your continued successes, I will gain strength. I give you the power to make masks of any spirit you come in contact with to gain their power. This is the most help I can be to you. In return, I ask that you believe in the spirits and me. Your path will take you where the spirits of science rule. Your powers will not wane even in the most heavily infested areas of science, but I may not be able to watch over you there. I am strongest among the people who remember me or in the wild places of the world that have rarely been touched by man," Old Broken Nose says as the silver shine on his eyes starts to fade. He inhales more mist from the pool and the sliver gleam returns. I can tell he is growing weary and will probably have to leave the Scarred One's body soon.

"How can I capture the Wendigo?"

"The wind has no home but Caleb does. Caleb is drawn to you and his home. If he cannot get to you, he will go home. There in the woods of your childhood, you can face him. Use the earth to trap him. I am strong in those woods and will help you as

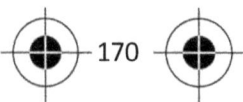

much as I can. But even if you capture him, you must be able to keep him caged until you find a cure. I do not have the strength to hold the Wendigo or cure him yet. The Raven and Coyote spirits were never trapped by the spirits of science and are still powerful and free. They can help but not until you appease them by finding their items of power. They can help cure Caleb but will not help to hold him. You may have to turn to the Cold Woman to contain the Wendigo until a cure can be found," Old Broken Nose says as the silver shine leaves his eyes completely. He falls to his knees and inhales more mist from the pool. He looks up at me and his eyes are barely silver. "My time is up. Take care Logan Longstride. I will watch your Eternal Hunt." With those last words, the silvery mist flows out of the Scarred One's nose and mouth in a torrent. It swirls around the room over to me. It covers me and I feel the cold of the mist as it envelopes me. Then it flows back into the pool.

The Scarred One is on all fours coughing. Wolf Watcher goes over to him and helps him recline as before we entered the cavern. The Scarred One lays back. He has stopped breathing and I can no longer hear his heartbeat. I guess our audience is over.

I look around. The werewolf I encountered in the woods is watching me with new interest. I wonder how much he witnessed of my meeting with Broken Nose?

Chapter 16:
Hidden Celebration

Later that night Amos and I are invited to attend a celebration honoring the spirits. We are given a hut by the cave of the Scarred One for the night. Wolf Watcher is constantly with us along with two warriors. The werewolf I encountered in the woods is often also around.

By everyone's behavior, I can tell that our status has changed. There is still a hint of caution but they have accepted us as part of the people, or one of their tribe. Our welcome by the Scarred One has made a big impact.

Wolf Watcher and the werewolf I encountered in the woods come to our hut before the night's celebration to talk. We sit outside in what little sun the massive trees allow. They, like everyone here, only speak to us in the Iroquois language.

"This is Moon Stalker. He says he has met you before, Logan," Wolf Watcher says.

"Yes, when I was hunting the Wendigo we crossed paths. Moon Stalker was also hunting the Wendigo," I say.

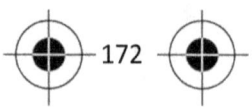

"That night I knew you smelled strange and of the spirits. I almost mistook you for the Wendigo," Moon Stalker says.

"You are a werewolf?" I ask looking at Moon Stalker. I can get a better look at him here in the daylight. He is of average height but powerfully built.

"Yes," Moon Stalker replies.

"Is everyone here a werewolf? Is that why you live in the old ways?"

"Most everyone here has the blood of the werewolf within them, but only a few of us are chosen by the spirits to become full werewolves," Moon Stalker says, gesturing for me to sit by the fire with him. He offers me a dipper of water, which I sip gratefully.

"We live in the old ways, as you call them, to be closer to the spirits. The way we live allows us to remain connected with our ancestral spirits. What Old Broken Nose told you was true. Many spirits have been trapped, driven away and weakened by the coming of science. Science tries to explain the magic out of the world. Science tries to put everything in neat little categories and boxes." Wolf Watcher says, pausing for a moment to let his words sink in before continuing. "Spirits would exist without people but they would be greatly diminished. They gain power from the belief of the people. They do not demand worship or service, just the belief that they exist. As the people stopped believing and science explained away our stories and legends, many spirits were lost to us." He takes back the cup and hands it to a young woman standing nearby. I smile at her in thanks.

"You have done a great thing in believing in Old Broken Nose. He has been freed to return to power because of your actions. Even by coming here and letting us hear your tale and see him speak through the Scarred One has greatly strengthened him. Now all of us know that Old Broken Nose is once again among the people. This is a great day!" Wolf Watcher exclaims, gesturing excitedly with his hands.

I feel the need to downplay my actions, since I'm the guest here. "I just did what I felt was right. What I felt I needed to do."

"That is the way of many great deeds. You did not start out to do something great, just to do what you felt was right and needed done. Your instincts led you down the right path," Wolf Watcher says. He motions towards the forest, making a sign like walking a path.

I consider what I've heard for a few moments but want to know more about this place and the people here. "I've never heard of this place. I'm surprised you can keep it hidden."

"Some of our people legally own all this land and more. This land is mostly a vast forest that is of little use to the modern world. Our warriors patrol the land

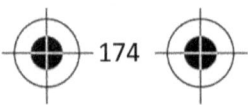

to keep strangers from wandering in. The spirits here are powerful enough to hide us from the satellites and planes that fly over. The spirits can even hold the tongue of most who would betray our secret. In these ways, we remain hidden and free from the outside world," Moon Stalker reveals. He offers to show us around the area and Amos and I follow him as he walks around the camp. Wolf Watcher joins us as we walk.

"Do your people live here all the time or do they go out into the world to see what is out there?" Amos asks.

"Almost all of our people go out into the modern world a couple of times a year. We have a place in a town near here where we send some of the children to be educated in the ways of the world. Some of them go on to college and beyond. Some even work in the world and only occasionally come here. Every once in a while, we even lose someone to the modern world. Those are times of great mourning for the people," Wolf Watcher explains.

"Are there other places like this in the world?" Amos asks.

"There are other hidden places where science is held at bay and the spirits are strong. There are other places where werewolves or other Spirit People live. We know of several and are on good terms with a few of them," Wolf Watcher says.

"Spirit People? What are they?" I ask.

"You are a Spirit Person because you have been touched by the spirits. Spirit People would be considered humans with supernatural abilities by the modern world. They are things like werewolves, fairies, vampires and immortals. There are also creatures that are obviously supernatural but were never human. Those types of creatures are not considered Spirit People," Wolf Watcher explains.

"Are you a Spirit Person?" I ask Wolf Watcher.

"Yes. I carry the blood of the werewolf in my veins even though I've never changed. This alone would make me a minor Spirit Person in our view. I am also a shaman who has been given the power to see and communicate with spirits. I can even enter the spirit realm. This power alone would make me considered a Spirit Person, even if I did not have werewolf blood," Wolf Watcher explains.

"What is the spirit realm?" I ask.

"The Spirit world is vast and made up of many different realms. The closest realm is the reflection of the world as we see it but with everything being alive with a spirit inhabiting it. So the tree, rock, mountain, animal, water, wind, would all be alive with a spirit. Each of these spirits can be interacted with if you know how. It is a place much more filled with life. Even locations like cities have a reflection in the spirit world and buildings, streets, computers, cars all have spirits. These are spirits of order and science, but they are spirits. There are a few of our people who have learned to talk to these spirits of order but I have never been able to. My ways are too traditional and nature focused to ever talk to a car," Wolf Watcher says, shaking his head like the whole idea is just wrong. He seems to be slightly annoyed at the idea of using technology.

"Oh, before I forget, I want to give your friend's knife back to you. You are welcome to wear it," Wolf Watcher says, and I know we have truly been accepted. He hands me Enuk's knife with a knowing look.

No sooner than I have Enuk's knife positioned a sound of wood upon wood, like a drum comes from all around. Wolf Watcher looks at us. "The ceremony is about to begin. We must go."

We all walk a short way to a clearing surrounded by huge evergreens. The trees all bend over the clearing to form a sort of roof. Only in the very center is there an opening to the sky about ten feet across.

In the middle of the clearing directly under the hole in the treetops is a grand bonfire. All around people eat, talk, play music, sing, dance and genuinely just enjoy themselves. Amos and I are given a place of honor by Wolf Watcher.

"If you fully want to participate in the ceremony, I recommend you drink this." Wolf Watcher holds up a gourd filled with a dark liquid. "This is spirit juice or simply spirits. I believe it was a misunderstanding about this drink and whisky that led to alcohol being called spirits. If you drink this you will be able to see into the spirit world."

I'm somewhat stunned. I've been through a lot of crazy stuff recently so I'm not sure why I am concerned about seeing into the spirit realm. Amos takes the gourd and drinks fully from it without a second thought. He hands it to me so I follow suit. It tastes sweet then very bitter. My tongue goes numb and feels strange in my mouth.

Then all the sudden, my view is filled with hundreds of silvery creatures. They are frolicking with the people in the clearing. They all look like real animals, plants or pieces of nature but they are surrounded by a silvery glow. Many are animals of the woods. There is a great bear that has to be three times bigger than any bear I ever even heard about. The treetops are filled with silvery birds of many varieties. Many of the birds are perched near a great bird that looks like a hawk. It has to be twelve feet from beak to tail and seems to flash with lightning. On the ground at the edge of the clearing, some children are playing with what I guess are rock spirits. They are chunky and somewhat clumsy. They can mold themselves into a crude human or animal shape, get up speed and then quickly roll around the ground by some magical means. The children try to catch them. It appears as if the spirits are really playing with the children.

The tree spirits are alive and moving about. They are huge, towering over the whole scene. I watch as a spirit tree steps right on top a group of people. They wave at the air and then move out from under it. At that moment, I understand I'm looking at an overlapped normal world and the spirit world. The tree spirit resides in the spirit world and consequently does not crush the people who exist in the real world. I guess real world is not right either since these spirits and their world is very real. My personal world view has been expanded.

All who have drunk the spirit juice can see the spirits and the spirits can see us. We can interact but not touch each other. I guess this is what I would be like to interact with ghosts. Are ghosts real to?

"Are the spirits we are seeing dead, like ghosts?" I resist the urge to try to touch a nearby spirit.

"Oh no. They are the true life of the forest. They reside inside and around their physical counterpart in our world. The spirits, animals or place it is associated with share a link. Depending upon how close the spirit world is in an area this connection can effect their counter part in the other world. If the animal is sick, the spirit could get sick. A strong spirit can help heal the animal. If a spirit inhabited a tree that was cut down, the spirit would become very weak as it wandered looking for another home. Spirits of the dead go to another level of the spirit world. The realms of the dead are many and mostly resemble man's belief," Wolf Watcher explains, gesturing around at different spirits as they dance and play.

"Can the spirits always see into our world?" I am blown way by all of this and have lots of questions.

"Some can, some can't. Some areas of our world are closely connected to the spirit realm so one can even walk between worlds. This is a place like that, so all the spirits can see into our world all the time. In other places, it may be very difficult to breach the walls of the spirit realm so the vast majority of the spirits cannot see into our world and it takes great effort for even a skilled shaman such as myself to peer into the spirit realm," Wolf Watcher says.

"Have you traveled in the spirit realm?" I ask.

"Oh yes, many times. It is a marvelous place that mimics our world in many ways. One can become lost and wander into the vast pathways that lead to the true spirit worlds. In those places our physical laws do not always apply and they can be very dangerous," Wolf Watcher says, with a scowl on his face obviously remembering some past encounter.

A small graceful woman approaches Wolf Watcher. Her white buckskin dress is ornately decorated with beadwork. She is a woman of great

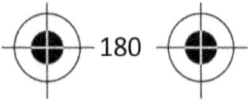

importance to be wearing such a garment. Her hair is as black as the single raven feather she wears in it. Her young skin is the slightly reddish brown of our people. She is strikingly beautiful.

Wolf Watcher stands up and greets the white clothed woman. "White Doe, you honor us with your presence. The spirits you have awoken prove you have the blood of your great grandfather, the Scarred One, in your veins."

"When I walked the realms the Scarred One was talking with Old Broken Nose. They spoke of one called Longstride. I have come to meet him," White Doe says looking from Wolf Watcher to me.

"White Doe, spirit-talker of the people, great granddaughter of the Scarred One, this is Logan Longstride," Wolf Watcher says, presenting me to her.

I bow and smile at White Doe. She nods at me, returning a graceful, gentile smile.

"Will you walk with me?" White Doe asks.

"Sure…umm…I would be honored," I say.

I follow White Doe away from the crowded clearing into the woods. I watch her walk with a grace I've rarely seen. She seems young to be treated with such respect. I bet she is not over eighteen and would not be surprised if she was only fifteen. White Doe slows and motions for me to walk beside her.

"I serve the spirits and my people. This is all I have known. I am one of the few who have never traveled to the outside world where science smothers belief," she says, looking ahead at the path and not me.

"Do you want to travel in the outside world?"

"I have traveled to many spirit realms and spied on the outside world from the spirit world. Someday I will walk among the lands of science, but I do not long for it," she says, still not looking at me.

I'm not sure how to act or what to say. White Doe has an honored place among the people that I do not really understand. She is very important to them. I wonder what she wants with me?

We continue to walk through the woods until even I, with my enhanced senses, can no longer hear the gathering. The silence grates on my nerves and I wish I could think of something to say.

We come to a small creek and White Doe leaves the path to walk upstream. The area is not very overgrown but I can tell it's rarely traveled even by animals. I start to see an abundance of spirits. Up ahead I hear water falling.

We come out of the woods into a small meadow by a pool formed at the base of a high waterfall. The water falls straight down some 20 feet into a rippling pool, and then continues downstream. This beautiful spot seems to be a focal point for local spirits.

White Doe takes my hand without looking at me. She leads me to the pool of water and steps upon it,

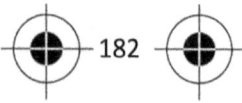

pulling me with her. Instead of the cold splash into the water I was expecting, we step into the silvery world of the spirits.

The entire landscape is outlined in a dim silvery glow. The spirits of animals are all around us. A deer spirit passes by me close enough to touch me and I'm startled by the feel of it. Its soft fur brushes my hand and feels almost real. No, not almost real. It feels more than real. Now that we are in the spirit realm, we can truly interact with the spirits.

I notice that some of the spirits glow differently than others. White Doe glows very brightly with an internal light. I even glow almost as brightly as she does.

"Why do some spirits glow brighter than others?" I ask, brushing my hands over an otter's back.

"It demonstrates their relative power, their life-force," she says.

"Why do you and I glow so brightly?"

"We both have powerful life-forces. Mine comes from being a werewolf and being chosen by the spirits as a shaman. Yours comes from your connection to Old Broken Nose and the Wendigo."

She leads me to a nice patch of grass. We sit together watching the waterfall and spirits roam around. She finally turns to me and looks me over as if she had not really seen me until now.

"Do you find it hard to serve the spirits?" she asks, her dark eyes penetrating.

"I never really thought about it. I want to help Caleb, and Old Broken Nose gave me the power to do that. I do not consider it service."

"My life has totally been about serving the spirits. I have spent more time in their company than with the people. Sometimes I wish I was not chosen by them and could just be a woman of the people." She looks a little melancholy at this thought, but it seems to pass quickly.

"Can't you be both?"

"I had hoped it would be that way but it seems that once again the spirits have other plans for me. I have always served the people by serving the spirits. I will continue to do so."

She looks at me and I can see sadness in her eyes. I want to help and comfort her but I do not know what I can do. She moves closer to me and kisses me. It's so slow and gentle. Her lips barely touch mine. She withdraws and looks in my eyes, searching for something. I move to kiss her and she closes her eyes. I kiss her deeply. She returns my attention and slowly our kissing becomes lovemaking.

I realize quickly that she is a virgin. We make love tenderly, with dozens of spirits around us. It's surreal and magical. After, we lay in each other's arms. White Doe begins to cry. I don't know what to do but just hold her.

"Is something wrong?" I ask, stroking her long soft hair.

"I cry for the life we will never live," she says, cuddling against my chest.

"The future is not set. How do you know what it will bring?"

"The spirits have told me. My place is here serving them. Your place is out in the world of men as a hunter."

"If you knew we were not going to be together why did you lie with me?"

"The spirits wished it."

I sit up and look at her. "You mean you had sex with me because the spirits told you to?"

"Yes."

"Do you do everything they tell you to do?"

"Yes. I serve the spirits. I always have. But now you have made me a woman and I will be alone when you leave." I don't think she understands how that sounds to me.

"I could come back?"

"Yes, you could, but I will be alone when you are gone. It does not matter, what is done is done. You must serve the spirits in your way and I will serve them in mine," she says, as she starts to get dressed.

"Look, we just went for a walk in the woods and one thing led to another. We never talked about any kind of commitment."

"I understand, Logan. I did this, not you. I lured you into the woods to lie with you," she says, turning away from me.

I put on my clothes. When we are both ready she grabs my hand and suddenly like a wave crashing over us, we are back in the normal world. She lets go of my hand and leads the way back to camp. We walk back together, but our silence forms a wedge between us.

At the edge of the celebration, White Doe stops and kisses me. It is a full kiss full of passion. It is a goodbye kiss.

"I will always remember you Logan Longstride. May your blade be sharp and swift," she says, as she disappears into the night.

I don't know what to think and I head back to my hut. I don't feel like joining in the celebration anymore.

Chapter 17:
Old Friends

The next morning Wolf Watcher and Moon Stalker take Amos and me back down the mountain and return our street clothes.

"Amos, it was good to meet you. You have a fine grandson there," Wolf Watcher says.

"I have always thought so," Amos says, grinning with pride.

"You are part of the people and welcome here anytime, Logan. The spirits will watch over you. Be safe," Wolf Watcher says.

"You have shown me a world I thought long forgotten. I'm proud to be a Seneca of the Iroquois people. Thank you for everything."

Moon Stalker eyes me as he walks over. He offers his hand. "Good hunting Logan Longstride," he says as we shake hands.

With our goodbyes said, we walk the last couple hundred yards alone. The SUV is parked at the trailhead with a very bored Hound at the wheel. He looks damn glad to see us. We climb in and the Hound heads out in a hurry.

"Agent Johansson wants you at the airfield ASAP," the Hound says.

"What's going on?"

"There has been another attack. She is already on the scene," the Hound says.

"After you drop me off, make sure Amos gets back to his hotel."

"Agent Johansson has already given me those orders."

I should have figured. Agent Johansson doesn't miss a thing.

Two hours later the chopper drops me off in what I think is a school parking lot. I'm met by a Hound who takes me to the scene of the attack. We drive through a small town. As I look around at all the houses, I realize the Wendigo is getting much bolder to attack so close to a large population.

The crime scene is just outside of the city limits in a few acres of woods. The traffic from the road can be heard but not seen from the house. It's a private enough place but not more than a quarter mile from town. Screams could have been heard from here. I'm surprised the Wendigo would choose this place.

When we pull up, I see Agent Johansson talking to a guy in a suit. The Suit is dressed, all in black, even his shirt and tie are black. His eyes are hidden behind black sunglasses. He looks to be in his mid to late thirties.

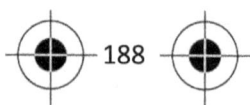

I stop dead in my tracks as Agent Johansson touches the Suit on the arm and actually smiles at him. They seem to be enjoying each other's company. I've never seen Agent Johansson smile, let alone touch anyone when she is working, except for that time she used a hug to place a bug on me. Who the hell is this guy?

I walk up and Agent Johansson notices me. Her smile vanishes as she snaps back into work mode. So maybe dealing with this guy is not work to her? Maybe they have a history?

"Logan, glad you could make it. This is Agent Smith," Agent Johansson says.

Agent Smith offers me his hand. "Nice to meet you, Logan. Glad to have you on the team."

"Nice to meet you," I say shaking Agent Smith's hand, but not really meaning it. I don't like how he makes Johansson smile.

"You can go over the crime scene if you like. It looks like it was our man," Agent Johansson says, turning back to Agent Smith.

"Umm...ok," I say as I walk towards the house, not liking how I'm being dismissed for some Suit.

In the first room, there are some bones that appear to have been gnawed on. I smell the death and decay of the bodies, but the smell is not quite right. There is also a sweet smell of strawberries in the air. I follow the sweet scent to the back of the house. There is a hot young thing kneeling on the hard wood floor. She has sexy short black hair. She is enthralled by something on the floor, but I can't see anything. Both her bare hands are pressed against the wood and she is staring at it entranced. I take the opportunity to admire her cute little ass while I wonder why she is breaking protocol and not wearing gloves.

She convulses and I think she might vomit. Instead she stands up and seems to notice me for the first time. Her momentary sickness fades from her face and I can see my first opinion was an understatement. This woman is super-hot.

"Hello? May I help you?"

It takes me a minute to stop staring into her dark blue mysterious eyes. "Umm…hi…I'm supposed to look at the crime scene," I say, not playing it near as cool as I would like.

"Well, it's pretty much all over so help yourself. I'm done here," she says, wiping her hands on her pants as if she is wiping off something icky.

"What do you think did this?" I ask, trying not to stare at her.

"You mean who? Who did this? Right?" she asks, as she picks up her bag.

"Yeah…umm…sorry. Who did this?"

"Sorry but I don't know who you are or how you relate to this case," she replies, starting to walk away. Cleary she intends to tell me nothing.

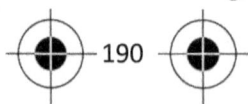

"I'm Logan, Logan Longstride. I work with Agent Johansson."

"I've heard about you," is all she says as she walks out.

I know I should probably look around more but I want to know who this mystery girl is, so I follow her out of the house. She walks right up to Agent Smith and Agent Johansson, but directs her conversation at Agent Smith.

"It was the lover of the wife. He made it look like the murders he had heard about in the news to cover his tracks. He is a copycat opportunity killer," the hot agent says.

"Are you sure about this?" Agent Johansson questions.

"If Becket says it, that's good enough for me," Agent Smith says, before the beautiful Becket can respond.

Agent Johansson nods her head in agreement to Agent Smith and the matter seems closed. I wonder who these other Agents are to be shown so much respect. This just seems so out of character for Agent Johansson.

"Logan, did you meet Becket? She is Agent Smith's partner," Agent Johansson says.

"We bumped in to each other inside," I say.

"Sorry we couldn't have been more help. We have another case that we have to get on or we would stay longer," Agent Smith says, looking at Agent Johansson.

"Maybe next time," Agent Johansson says, almost purring.

Agent Johansson and Agent Smith walk off towards the cars talking. I take the opportunity to talk to Becket. "Are you a profiler?"

"Something like that," she says, being FBI agent vague.

"How long have you been an Agent?" I ask, just trying to keep the conversation going.

"Long enough to know you aren't an Agent yet. But I heard you are going to sign up. Hope you catch your man."

"Oh I will." I look over at Agent Johansson being familiar with Agent Smith. "Have they worked together before?"

"I'm pretty sure they have some kind of history. Agent Smith is normally not this friendly."

"Yeah, I know what you mean. Agent Johansson is usually ice cold when she's on the job."

We stand there together watching our partners. They show each other an intimacy that I guess we have not earned. I bet they were lovers or at least in love with each other once. They look so at home together. It kind of pisses me off.

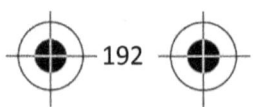

I look back at Becket. Her profile is radiant in the afternoon sun. I want to know more. "What case are you working on?"

"Down south, there are some bloodsuckers that are leaving a trail of bodies," Becket says, as if it's just a normal case.

"Umm…by bloodsucker, you mean vampire, right?"

Becket looks at me with her deep blue eyes. "Wow! You are new! Yes, I mean vampires. Why don't you fill me in about your case."

"My cousin, Caleb, was trapped in a cabin for six weeks without food. He became a cannibal to survive. He was then cursed and taken over by a Wendigo spirit. Now he is killing and eating humans. I'm trying to capture him so I can remove the curse."

"I knew about the Wendigo but not how it related to you. Sorry for your loss. The personal cases are always the worst," Becket says, and I can tell she knows from first-hand experience.

Agent Smith waves us over. He is already heading to his car.

"Well I will see you around. Be safe," Becket says, as she heads for her car.

"Yeah, see ya around."

I walk over to Agent Johansson. I watch her face grow long as her eyes follow Agent Smith leave.

"How do you know Agent Smith?"

"We used to be partners," Agent Johansson says, but I know there is definitely more to the story than that.

"Let's go, Logan. It's time you became one of us."

Chapter 18: H.E.L.

On the chopper ride, I begin to feel apprehensive about joining Agent Johansson's organization. After talking to Old Broken Nose, I'm not sure if this is the right path for me anymore. However, I can't discount that Agent Johansson's organization has information, manpower, equipment, cash and an ability to cut through the red tape. All of these things would be useful to have but at what cost.

"Where are we going?" I finally ask, more to think about something else than anything.

"To our main facility in the northwest," Agent Johansson says, yelling over the noise of the chopper.

"Are we flying into the USA?"

"Very good, Logan. The base is a little south of the Canadian border. It serves as a hub for the missions west of the Rockies and north into Canadian and Alaska."

"So am I going to swear an oath and get a badge or something?" I look below at the rugged landscape.

"It is a little more complicated than that," Agent Johansson's annoyed stare tells me there is more.

"One more thing Logan, you must always assume that everything you say or do will be heard and seen."

I watch Agent Johansson and feel she just gave me a warning. I thought these people were the good guys. Why would I need to watch what I say or do?

We fly along the east side of the Rockies so I figure we are in Montana. The helicopter lands in a large valley, close to a sheer stone cliff. There are several cabins and a lodge that are pretty well concealed by thick tree cover.

Right after the helicopter lands, I'm startled by a sideways jerk. As the engine powers down, we are being moved along the ground into the rock wall on some kind of conveyor belt like a kiddie ride at an amusement park. As we are about to hit the wall, a huge door opens up and we pass into a hidden facility. Right after we clear the door it closes again.

The hanger we are in has ten bays for helicopters, six of which are full. Most are black military choppers used primarily for transport but two are full-fledged attack choppers with missiles and guns all over them. I wonder what kind of supernatural threat gets that kind of attention.

We continue to move on the conveyer mechanism down the main hanger and then into a bay. There is a support crew and some security Hounds going about their business. Further in is a large area for ground vehicles that is mostly full. This place is way more

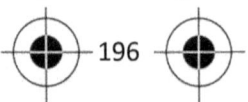

hidden and high tech than I expected. I wonder if they are trying to hide from supernaturals or normal people or maybe both?

Agent Johansson motions to all of this. "Welcome to HEL Logan. That is HEL spelled H, E, L. It stands for Hunters of Eternal Lies."

"HEL, really? I'm going to work in HEL?" I say, mostly to myself in disbelief as I try to take it all in as we walk further into the facility.

"HEL is the name we use internally. It's never to be used outside the Agency. When you are in the field, you will have several active identities with all the credentials to back them up," Agent Johansson says, leading me down the hanger.

I look at the Hounds walking around and realize the joke. They are the Hounds of HEL. The name Hounds makes more sense to me now. Whoever created this organization must have had a sick sense of humor.

At the rear of the hanger/garage, we enter an elevator. The doors shut and an animatronic voice squawks out of a speaker. "Identify yourself."

"Agent Johansson and Logan Longstride," Agent Johansson says.

Agent Johansson then looks into a viewer, I can see her eyes caught on a screen, and overlapped by images that I figure are pictures of her eyes that are on file. I have to do the same but mine are not compared to anything.

Agent Johansson next places her thumb on a pad and quickly draws it away. She motions for me to do the same. I place my thumb in the depression and look over at Agent Johansson who has her thumb in her mouth. The pain of the prick in my finger comes as I realize this is a blood test. Maybe they are testing for supernatural blood or matching our DNA to our file.

I figure that is it, until Agent Johansson puts on her sunglasses and tells me to close my eyes. The elevator is flooded with extremely bright light that I catch a millisecond of before I close my eyes. Even through my eyelid, I can see the brightness of the light. After about a minute, the light fades back to normal and the elevator starts moving.

There are six floors below the garage level we entered and one floor above for a total of eight buttons. Agent Johansson pushed the third one down or the first underground level. I guess we are descending into HEL, I chuckle to myself.

"This place is huge. Why is it so big?"

"This is a HEL home base. There are only a handful of bases like this in the world. Most government facilities are known and therefore somewhat unsafe. A home base is unknown and we go to great lengths to keep it that way. Here we have

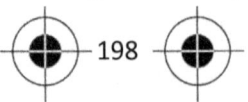

the facility to do proper research and development. That takes a lot of people and space. The people who work here also live here for extended periods of time."

The elevator door opens and a scrawny little woman is standing in front of us. She looks me over as I appraise her. Her shoulder length brown hair is flat and unflattering. Her features are sharp and angular. She seems to be in her early thirties but gives the impression of being more like an old woman who is wasting away. She is just rail thin. I bet she is not even five feet tall but her huge heels give her a boost. She is holding a notepad computer with a touch screen.

When she is done inspecting me, she smiles in a way that makes me feel uneasy. She has the grin of a starving cat that just caught a nice juicy mouse.

"Logan Longstride, you will follow me," the twig of a woman says.

Before I can start following the small woman, Agent Johansson speaks. "Really, Regina is all this formality necessary? Logan is with me." Agent Johansson places her hand on my arm to stop me from getting off the elevator.

Regina whirls around and fixes her gaze on Agent Johansson. I can see the hate and fury in her eyes. "It is my job to escort people to the director. Mr. Longstride will come with me," Regina almost yells.

Regina turns around and starts down the hall obviously expecting me to follow her. I look at Agent Johansson who almost grins at me. I can see she likes tormenting this tiny woman.

Agent Johansson follows Regina and I follow her. We go just a short distance and Regina turns to motion me into a conference room. Her expression flashes rage when she sees Agent Johansson leading me into the room. She pounds away on her electronic note pad with her stylus, probably lodging some complaint about Agent Johansson.

The conference room is big enough for twenty people to sit comfortably around a large oval table. The walls and tabletop are all screens that I figure work as video and computers. At the end of the table are four men.

The man at the head of the table is in his forties. He looks like the many politicians that came to speak to my tribe. His suit is dark blue, his tie a vibrant red. Everything is pressed and tailored to fit. His black hair is short and I bet cut every week. His face is round and a little boyish. His hands are manicured and skin moisturized. He looks like he has never done a hard days labor in his life.

Before I can really get a good look at the others, the politician speaks. "Good afternoon Logan. I am Director Kenneth Mott. I am in charge of this facility. I want to be the first to welcome you to our

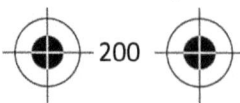

organization. Agent Johansson has spoken very highly of you and I look forward to having you on the team. For now, you will continue to report to Agent Johansson."

"I know this must all seem a little overwhelming right now but as time passes you will settle in. I try to run a tight operation that follows the rules. The most important rules are the following. One, you never divulge information about the HEL organization to those outside the organization. Two, you support your fellow HEL members. And three, you will share all information with our HEL organization and not keep secrets about supernaturals to yourself."

"There are other rules but-" Mott cuts off as Regina coughs, then starts back up after glancing at her. "Ah…another rule is always fill out your reports neatly and get them in on time." Mott seems to have lost his place after Regina's interruption. "Well that is enough from me for now. I want you to meet the other heads of staff."

On cue, the very pale man to Mott's left begins to speak. His white hair is scraggly and going every which way. He is dressed in a crisp white lab coat that looks to be much better taken care of than his personal hygiene. "I am Horst Stecher, head of research. I hope you are more a man of science than the woman of action who is your partner. Please remember that we find out much more from live subjects than dead ones. And more from slightly damaged bodies than from exploded hunks," Stecher says, glaring at Agent Johansson who just shrugs her shoulders.

"If you find anything in the field that you think we may have interest in please send it on. If you are not sure, then send it in. The smallest thing can sometimes lead to a great discovery. We will never be able to win without the knowledge of what we are truly up against."

I'm not sure if Stecher is done or not but he paused long enough for the man on Mott's other side to begin speaking. "Luc Lesage, cleaner. You make the mess, I clean it up." I study Luc and wonder if he is going to say more but I doubt it. He is not a tall man but very stocky. I bet he is really strong. His face shows sign of being repeatedly cut and bruised. His nose has the obvious signs of being broken more than once. His fingers are so huge and beat-up that they look like sausages wrapped in sandpaper.

The last man in the room I already know. He is the epitome of the young military man. "Scott North, security chief. Logan and I've already worked together," Scott says.

The Director then begins to talk again. "One more thing. I do have an open door policy. I would ask you to try to deal with Agent Johansson on any issues you may have. But if you need to talk to me personally

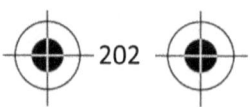

feel free to stop by." I feel like a schoolboy standing in front of the principal.

With that, the introductions seem to be over. Mott stands and the others follow suit, and file out of the conference room. Only Regina stays behind. I watch as she plops a large stack of paperwork on the table.

"Here are the files we need to go over to get you instated as an agent. It will probably take some time," she says, looking menacingly at Agent Johansson.

"I'll stand by your side in front of a horde of monsters but paperwork is another matter. Have short stuff here call me when you're done," Agent Johansson says, as she gets up and leaves.

Regina is crushing her pen as she glares at Agent Johansson leaving the room. I consider asking what the deal is between them but think that would be a very bad idea. Anyway, if I'm going to ask, I should ask Agent Johansson.

The paperwork is tedious but as I'm nice to Regina, she is nice to me. By the end of the stack of papers needing my signature, I can tell Regina really likes me. She even puts her hand on my arm and scoots her chair over close to mine. It kind of creeps me out.

When we are done, she just sits with me chatting, I start to wonder what her motives are. Five, ten then fifteen minutes pass and we are still chatting with her hand on my arm. I want to get on with it and not just sit and chat to this creepy little woman. So I ask if she can call Agent Johansson.

"I see how you are. You are like all the rest only interested in her." Regina snatches up her paperwork and stomps towards the door. She wobbles on her high heels and for a second I'm sure she is going to fall. She mumbles to herself as she leaves the room. "I am more of a woman than that blond bimbo…"

I sit stunned and alone in the conference room. I guess, I figured a powerful secret agency like HEL would run like clockwork. Well then, maybe Regina is the cuckoo.

I call Agent Johansson and she stops by to get me. "Come on Logan, I can show you around a little. You don't have high enough security rating to see the really good stuff yet."

"How do I get a better security rating?" I say, running a little to catch up.

"Time served mostly. But sometimes you work on a case that kind of thrusts secrets into your lap. Kind of like this case, where you know more about Wendigos than anyone else around here."

"Do you have a high security rating?" I already think I know the answer. I just want to see what she says.

Agent Johansson just glances at me before replying. "Yes."

"How long have you worked for HEL?"

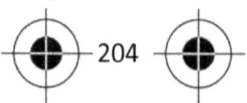

"Six years. I was recruited straight out of high school to join the CIA as a field agent. After a few years, I was on a case that brought me into contact with supernaturals. After that I was approached and recruited into HEL," Agent Johansson says as she slowly turns the engagement ring on the wrong hand.

I bet she has never lived a normal life. Being plucked right out of high school into a world of lies and spies. Her ring speaks of a life that could have been but is no longer even conceivable. I hope I can keep enough distance between the job and home to have a personal life. I should go home to my family, to Jessy. Maybe joining HEL was a mistake, but it's too late now.

Chapter 19:
Changing Tactics

A coupleof days later, we go to investigate a possible Wendigo attack. The crime scene is in southern Canada. If this is the Wendigo then, it looks to be heading straight for its home, my home.

The crime scene is a house off the beaten path. The home is a real nice brick two story. I see a swing set, bikes, a trampoline and my heart sinks. I have been around a lot of death in the last couple of weeks but kids. I don't know if I can handle looking at dead kids.

I wander around the property hoping to find something that points to the Wendigo so I don't have to go inside. Agent Johansson goes straight inside to look around. I guess dead kids don't even faze her anymore. Hell, she was almost a kid herself when she started working for the government. I can see her as a CIA spook. I bet she got into places many male agents couldn't. She is one of the most beautiful women I've ever seen and I bet she was even hotter when she was younger. Her marks never stood a chance.

But Agent Johansson is much more than a pretty face. I can tell that she has succeeded in a male

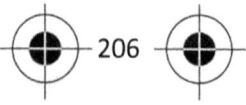

dominated world. I bet she not only wanted to be as good but better than the guys. She sure grew into one competent woman.

A faint scent of death calls my attention back to the task at hand. I follow the scent and find a track, then another. The Wendigo stood right here and watched the people of the house go about their normal lives. It fought the hunger within its gut long enough to admire its meal. The thought of my blood brother Caleb being capable of not only killing a child but also eating her nearly makes me sick.

Agent Johansson calls to me. I welcome the distraction, as I was about to spill my breakfast upon the ground. My stomach still churning, I walk over to the front of the house to talk to Agent Johansson.

"Not a pretty sight inside. It looks like the work of the Wendigo," Agent Johansson says. "I'm sorry but I have to ask you to go see if it truly was the Wendigo, Logan."

"Oh, it was the Wendigo. I found some tracks and it's scent over there," I say, pointing to the spot.

"Ok. Do you know which way it went and how long ago?"

"South. I would guess a good twelve hours ago. I'm pretty sure it's heading home. I must go and prepare a trap for it." I can feel the fear for my family starting to build inside me. I need to protect them.

"What is your plan?"

"First I'm going alone," I say quickly and continue before Agent Johansson can object. "I want to do this my way. I know what to do and will get the job done."

As she starts to protest, I interrupt. "Look, this is my home we are talking about. I only joined up with HEL because I was promised I could keep my private life. If we go into my home with a bunch of armed men, my family will never be the same. I need to keep my home and work separate. I promise I will keep you informed and hope you will be standing by for my call if I need back up," I say.

"I don't like it, Logan. I understand what you are saying, but if you mess up, your whole family could be killed. Have you thought about that?" she replies, irritation on her face.

"If my family dies, I will have already given my life trying to protect them. I have to try this my way. Will you please help me?"

"If you will promise to wear a panic button at all times...I guess." Before she can say any more I wrap my arms around her in a great big hug. She tenses at the public display of affection. "Logan there are people watching..." and I release her. She looks unmoved by my hug and moves to distance herself from me. She goes over to one of the Hounds and barks orders at him.

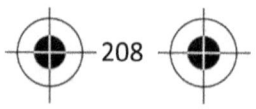

I watch as Agent Johansson takes her discomfort out on the innocent Hounds under her command. It seems strange to me that she can be perfectly calm while being stalked by a supernatural threat and then so unnerved by a simple hug. With Agent Smith she was familiar, smiling and there was even some body contact. Why should me hugging her receive such a harsh reaction? We have slept together twice. She has rejected my recent sexual advances but I just figured that was because we are busy. Maybe it's something more? Something I do not understand?

"Time to go Logan," one of the Hounds yells to me, bringing me back to the moment.

Before we head out Agent Johansson gives me a watch that I have to promise to never take off until the Wendigo is caught. Along with being a timepiece it has a compass, GPS, also serves as a panic button, and a cell phone that only calls Agent Johansson. It probably has a toothpick and a bottle opened too.

****

My plans for going home are cut short by a phone call. Just to the south of the last attack another one is reported through a 911 call. We are still in the area so are going to try to intercept the Wendigo. Agent Johansson calls for back up and we head south. After a three hour drive we are on the scene. Our black SUV is joined by two others and a chopper. Our force consists of Scott, Agent Johansson, nine Hounds on the ground and another four in the chopper.

The attack was at a mansion out in the woods. The place has to be over 6000sqft with a multilevel wrap around deck. The house is a log cabin lodge style. The wife ran to their panic room and locked herself in when she heard the Wendigo attack. Even so she was not safe. Looking at the door it is amazing to me the amount of hunger that would drive the Wendigo to spend so much time ripping through the steel door to the panic room. All the while the wife frantically crying to 911 for help.

Help did come but it was too late. Both bodes were stripped clean of flesh and even some bites were taken out of the larger bones that look to be for sucking out the marrow. I have seen grisly kill sights where a pack of wolves has eaten a moose that look a lot tidier than this bloodbath. The hunger must have been driving the Wendigo mad for such a scene.

It is just after midnight and the trail is three hours old. The moon is half full and the terrain rugged and tree covered. Agent Johansson remembers well the last time we set out to hunt the Wendigo at night and wants to wait until first light.

"Let me go. I can move a lot faster and will be in constant contact with you through my nifty G-man watch."

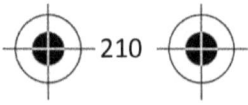

"What if it attacks you? Even if we are following in the chopper and SUVs, it will take time to get to you."

"Keep me updated to where you are and I can bring it to you."

"It could kill you before you make it to us."

"That is a possibility...but I know the Wendigo. I will make it."

"Fine. But you keep me up to date. We can follow you with the GPS in your watch.

After getting geared up, I head out. The first thing I do is use the sent glands of an Elk on myself that I had collected for just such an occasion. The Wendigo will hopefully only smell an Elk and not a human as I come upon it.

It takes me a couple of minutes to get past the Elk scent on myself so I can catch a whiff of the deathly stale air of the Wendigo. Slowly at first I move into the woods. I open my senses and feel the forest. The wind is still and smells of a grave. Animals are silent and hidden. The Wendigo must be close.

"It's still in the area...be ready," I whisper into my mic.

Following a trace of a game trail, I head deeper into the woods. It winds along a ravine that I can hear contains a babbling brook. The trees are strong, tall pines that block most of the sun, so the undergrowth is sparse and easily navigated.

My movements are slow and calculated. A few steps taking care not to disturb anything that might carry sounds of my location. Then short pauses where I force my senses in to my surroundings searching for anything out of place. It is often a sound or movement that seems innocent but is out of place that warns the hunter or the prey.

After an hour, I have worked my way a couple of miles down the ravine. The lights from the house are dim and only occasionally visible through the dense foliage. I stop and listen. The babble of the brook comes to my ears but something is not quite right. Where it was a consistent rhythmic chaos of water upon rock, there is also an emptiness. This happens four times and then it stops. I am still as the tree I am leaning against as my eyes search the area for what could have made the anomaly.

Then I see it. The Wendigo is moving slowly up the other side of the ravine. It's path will bring it out of the brook. Those sounds I heard must have been its steps in the water. It moves carefully as a hunter stalking its prey. I watch unmoving as it climbs further up the ravine to a rock outcropping. There it perches in a crouched animalistic posture and looks back towards the scene of it's recent meal. I'm sure it can see the house from its vantage point.

The light of the half-moon comes out from behind a meandering cloud and gives me a better look at my

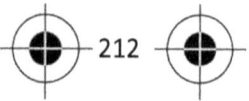

quarry. Shock grips me, as the emancipated form of a man is clearly visible. Its skin is splattered with dark splotches that I know are the blood of my friends from Bear Ridge as well as its other victims. Hell, some of that blood is even my own. Then I remember that some of it is also his blood, which I have spilled during battle.

Caleb stands erect as a man and the patch of his white hair catches the moonlight. This thing that I try over and over to make a monster is my cousin, my blood brother. The Wendigo spirit may be pulling the strings but somewhere deep inside Caleb still lives.

Caleb raises his head to the sky and lets out an unearthly wail that sounds like an evil wind passing through a narrow canyon. The sounds makes a chill run down my spine.

"I'm sorry Caleb, but it has to stop," I whisper to myself.

"Target spotted half a klick to the east from my location. I will try to bring it to you."

"Understood, Logan," Agent Johansson says through my earpiece.

I study the terrain for the best way back to the house. I will have to be running at full speed to keep away from the Wendigo. There is not really an ideal path but I see a couple ways that don't look too bad. I pick up a baseball-sized rock. I take in a deep breath and wing it right at the Wendigo. The rock misses but does manage to hit the stone outcropping, causing a loud noise.

The Wendigo goes prone as it searches for its attacker. I unsheathe Enuk's knife and move it back and forth, so that it catches the moon light. The Wendigo sees my signal and stares at me with its cold dead eyes. It bends its head back and lets out its unearthly wail, "WaaEee!" Before leaping down and coming right at me. Part of me wants to just stand here and meet it in bloody battle to the death, but then I remember Jessy and Faith and the rest of the people counting on me. So I turn and run back toward the house and the awaiting hounds.

"Logan, we heard it's howl. Are you alright?" Agent Johansson asks, with a little hint of concern in her voice.

"Kind of busy right now. Bringing it to you," I manage to say through heavy breaths as I run.

"All teams ready weapons, contact at any moment. Wait for Logan to get clear before you engage," Scott says through my ear mic.

I am running as fast as I can, but I can feel the Wendigo closing on me. I am almost back to the clearing behind the house. If I can just get the Wendigo into the open, we might have a chance.

PAIN! And wet from my back overwhelm my senses. I do everything I can to keep running. I can see the clearing. Help is moments away.

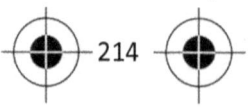

Before I can even take another step, a huge weight pushes me to the ground and I tumble, tangled up with the Wendigo. My fall might have just saved my life, as I make it to my feet the same time as the Wendigo. We slowly move in a circle eyeing each other. The Wendigo is snarling and showing me its sharp, once human teeth. I am just trying to block out the pain of the wounds on my back so I can judge when I am closest to the clearing. My goal is to make a break for it as soon as I can.

The back of my shirt is totally wet and sticking to my skin. As the top of my jeans start to get soaked, I know I am in trouble. I am not sure how much more blood loss I can take. I have to go now.

Faking a lunge at the Wendigo, I dart off toward the clearing. The Wendigo lets out a wail and follows. Those precious moments give me the lead I need to make it into the clearing. "It's here!" I yell into my mic.

The Wendigo follows me right out into the clearing, closing fast.

"Down! Logan, down now!" Scott yells and I drop down into the grass.

Scott gives the order, "Open fire!" And the air comes alive with automatic weapon fire.

The noise is deafening as even the chopper closes in and opens up with it's chain guns. I cover my ears and hope I'm far enough away from the Wendigo to be safe. Right as the thought goes through my mind I feel a hot sting in my leg and then another.

I scream into my mic, "Ahhh!"

"Cease fire! Cease fire! Friendly is being hit," Agent Johansson orders.

Almost immediately the shooting stops. I look over at the crumpled heap that was once my cousin, Caleb. His body looks more like a pile of hamburger than anything vaguely human.

"Team A, converge on target and confirm the kill. Team B, extract Logan from target area," Scott orders.

A couple Hounds grab me and carry me off to the road. As a medic is looking me over, the wind shifts. I look up and see clouds moving over the house from all directions.

"Target is just a piece of meat," a Hound reports. "Will bag and tag it."

"NO!" I say. "It's still alive. Get out of there."

"Logan? What is it?" Agent Johansson asks.

"Look at the clouds. It's gathering strength. You need to get your men out of there."

"I don't know what he's talking about ma'am. Nothing could have survived this," a Hound reports.

"Burn it! Burn it all," Agent Johansson orders.

"Dr. Stecher wants as much evidence as possible, ma'am," the Hound says.

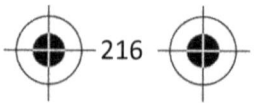

"Stecher be dammed. You do what I say, or I will deal with you personally. BURN it NOW!" Agent Johansson orders.

"Yes, ma'am," the Hound says.

Then another Hound speaks up, "Did you see that?"

"See what?" the first Hound asks.

"That! See it's moving," the second Hound says.

"BURN IT!" Scott and Agent Johansson scream into their mics.

I see a flash of light, which I know, has to be a Blaster. Then my earpiece explodes with the screams of multiple Hounds.

The air erupts with automatic weapon fire that moves off into the woods. Then the forest flashes white. It takes me a moment to feel the concussion wave of the rockets blowing huge craters in the woods.

All most as fast as the firing started it stops. "Report," Scott orders. Each team reports in with the same response, "Contact lost."

Chapter 20: Going Home

A few days later, after my wounds have healed, we take a chopper close to my home near Salamanca, NY. I'm dropped off near my car and released to make my preparations for the Wendigo. Agent Johansson and a team of Hounds will be standing by for my signal to move in. The containment cell is being flown in from the HEL facility in Montana and will be here in a day or two.

"I will try to hold off HEL for as long as I can but I doubt you have more than a couple of weeks." Agent Johansson takes off her shades so I can see her eyes before continuing. "If the body count gets much higher this case could be taken out of my hands and given to the cleaners."

"I understand. Thanks for giving me the chance."

"Good luck, Logan. Stay alive. I don't want Regina screaming at me about all the paper work she will have to do if you die," Agent Johansson half smiles to me.

"I'll do my best," I say as the chopper takes off, grinning back at her.

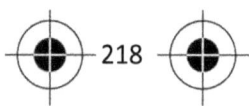

In forty-five minutes, I am pulling up in front of Jessy's house. I'm glad to see her car in the drive. I consider walking up to the front door but do not want to go through the whole parent thing. I decide to go around back to the window I've used for years to get in and out of Jessy's basement.

The window is wide open as it's a nice spring day. I'm about to climb in when my heightened senses detect the mixed odors of sex. At first anger overwhelms me. Who the hell is Jessy sleeping with?

I fall back into a sitting position before the open window. Part of me wants to go inside and confront her. Hell all of me wants to. I climb through the window all ready to get in a big fight with Jessy and beat the crap out of whoever she is with. It had just better not be that damn Phillip Little prick. I round the corner and bump right into Jessy's naked mom. I don't know which of us is more startled. She covers her breasts with her hands and screams.

I don't know what to do. I guess I should look away but I'm just so stunned to see Jessy's naked mom. I was so prepared to find Jessy with another man that I never considered it would be her parents having sex in the basement. I'm still staring at Jessy's mom when a naked man enters the room. It takes me a second to realize he's holding a pistol and it's pointed at me. The naked man is not only not Jessy's dad, but is Harry Wilson, the local Caucasian sheriff.

"Is Jessy home?" I ask as casually as I can.

"She's at work. She drove my car. Hers is acting up," Jessy's mom stammers.

"All righty then. I'll go see her there," I say, turning to leave.

"Logan!" The sheriff yells to stop me, but I keep walking. This time I walk up the stairs and out the front door of the house.

Ten minutes later, I'm in front of the Little Pub where Jessy works. I go inside and am startled to see my mom sitting in a booth with a man twice her age. He looks to be well off from his suit. There are several empty glasses in front of my mom and she is guzzling on a drink as I watch. It turns my stomach to see my mom this way.

The man has his hands all over my mom. She is so drunk, she seems to hardly notice. I don't understand how she has let herself fall so far. I am about ready to storm over when Jessy's hand on my shoulder distracts me. I turn and look into her bright blue eyes. Her smile washes over me like the warm summer sun filling me with an inner warmth.

Jessy kisses me and I fall into her. All that exists is her. I crush her in my arms as our tongues dance together. Her familiar scent surrounds me like her loving arms. All is right in the world again.

"Logan...you...are...hurting me..." Jessy whispers and I release my grip on her.

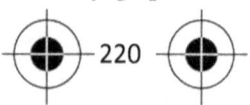

"I'm sorry, Jess. I'm just glad to see you."

"I missed you too, Logan. Let's go outside where we can talk," she says pulling me with her.

I enjoy being led out of the pub by Jessy until the images of my mom come flooding back into my head. I glance back to make sure I didn't imagine it and sure enough, there she is kissing some old dude. Anger surges through me but Jessy manages to get me outside.

"Calm down Logan. Look at me," Jessy says, as she turns me so my back is to the bar.

"Does my mom come her a lot?" I ask through clenched teeth.

"Sometimes. You know how she is. Why are you so surprised?"

Her question rather stuns me. "I guess I know what she does and have even seen it a couple times. But she is my mom. She used to be such a good mom. So it shocks me and frankly pisses me off each and every time I see her like this. It makes me want to go up to her and shake her. And say, *What the hell are you doing? You have a daughter at home who needs you. Get your shit together and come home to your family.*"

Jessy hugs me. "I wish it was that easy," she says. "My mom has come home a couple times recently really drunk. I don't know what to do. My dad just sits there in shock when it happens."

"I hate to be the one to tell you, but I stopped by your house first. I caught your mom and sheriff Wilson together."

"You mean like really together? Like they were having..." Jessy cannot even finish the sentence as she is so overwhelmed by tears.

I hold her tight. It's better to get it all out at once. There has to be no mistake in her mind as to what I meant. "They were naked and had been having sex. I'm so sorry, Jess."

"How did our lives get so screwed up? Is this the future we have in store? Am I going to become like my mom and turn to the bottle and the arms of someone outside our family? I hate this place. Everyone is all up in everyone else's business. I feel trapped when I'm here. Smothered by the disapproving looks of the pure bloods when they see my blue eyes and from the whites who only see another damn Indian. Let's go away, Logan. Will you take me away from this place?"

I know Jessy doesn't mean everything she is saying, but a lot of it's true. She has never fit in as well as I did, but I'm of a very pure and respected family. My grandparents have been the example I have always looked to for how families should be. This has given me a grounding even when my mother left. Also, when she left I was already at college so I didn't have to live the day-to-day drama that played out. My family did not burden me with what was happening because they wanted me to concentrate on school and beginning my own life.

"It will be ok Jessy. I know it doesn't seem like it now but it will be ok. Why don't you come stay with me tonight?"

"I would like that. I don't think I could face my mother right now."

Right then the door to the Little Pub opens and my mom stumbles out on the arm of the old dude. I turn and watch them coming closer and closer to us. I step in front of their path and my mom squints through bloodshot eyes to see me.

"Orrin? Is that you? Have you come to collect me again, well just don't…I'm just fine with…um…" she starts to whisper. "What's your name sweetie?"

"Um…Bob," the old guy says unsurely.

"Yeah…Bob is taking good care of me." She points and then pokes her finger repeatedly into my chest as she continues to talk. "I don't need the likes of you Orrin, coming around here and spoiling all my fun. You just go home and don't come back."

"I'm not Orrin. I'm your son, Logan."

"Logan? He was such a good little boy. You can't be Logan. You're a man," my mom says.

"You have lost a lot of time in the bottle, mom. I've grown up. I'm Logan, your son."

"Logan is that really you? Look Bob, it's my little boy all grown up. See how he looks like his father, Orrin." My mom comes closer and touches my face.

"Let's go home mom. Faith is waiting for you."

"Faith, my precious Faith. I would like to see my little girl."

I take my mother's hand and see Bob considering what to do. I glare at him and he decides the best thing is to skulk off. We go to my car and I help my mother in the passenger seat.

"Jessy you coming?" I ask as I walk around and get in.

"Yeah Logan, I am," Jessy says smiling at me with tears in her eyes. "Let me clock out and I'll come over."

My mom puts her head on my shoulder and falls asleep on the short ride to our house. My dad is on the porch when I pull up. I know he is surprised to see me but is downright stunned when I help Sally, my mom out of the car. I watch as my dad's face lights up with a hope I rarely see in him anymore. I have to hold my mom steady, as she is still pretty drunk.

I bring her around so she can see Orrin, my father, her husband and our home. She starts to cry and thrash against me. "No, don't make me. Please…not here," she says, becoming dead weight in my arms as she starts crying

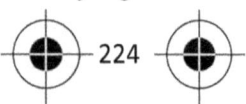

I pick my mom up and carry her over to my father. I sit her in a chair next to my father's wheelchair. He takes her hand and kisses it. She falls into his lap crying.

"I'm so sorry, Orrin. Sorry for everything. You are more a man without your legs than any man I've ever met. I'm so sorry. Please forgive me," my mom cries.

My dad just hugs her. From what I've heard things like this have happened before and my mom always leaves a couple of days later. This has to be hard on my dad. I can't imagine what he is going through.

"Oh Sally, I just want you home. I want my wife back. The mother of our children back," my dad manages to get out before he starts crying to.

It's strange to watch my mother and father together at all, let alone crying uncontrollably. I stand by and just let their reunion happen. I don't know if it will last but at least my mother is home for now.

Jessy pulls up and I walk out to meet her. I hold her as we both watch my parents clinging to each other weeping. The pain of the years they have been apart is all coming out in their tears. It's a soul-crushing thing to watch.

"God, I've never seen anything like this," Jessy says, squeezing me a little tighter.

"It's heartbreaking," I say as I watch my parents. I made this happen and I have to see it through. Right then I make a decision. "I'm not going to let her leave this time. I don't know how but I will make my mother come home for good this time."

Jessy looks at me searching my eyes. "I don't know if even you can make her choose to stay home. Your dad has always just let her choose her own path."

I set my jaw stubbornly. "Well maybe my father was wrong. Maybe my mom needs some help choosing what is right for her family."

"It's is a dangerous thing you are messing with," Jessy says, laying her hand on my cheek. "If she is really unhappy here, things will get ugly, especially if you force her to stay. You don't want Faith to see her mom break down again."

"You are right about Faith. She may have to go live with our grandparents till this is worked out," I sigh and start to think harder about what I am planning.

Jessy tries to reason with me again. "You are pushing really hard and you don't even know if there will be a problem. Slow down Logan. Things like this have to have time to heal. It has been four years since your mom left. Not everything can be fixed overnight or with force. Your mom needs to feel safe and loved. You cannot make her home a prison and expect her to

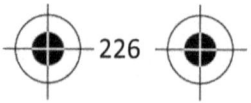

want to stay. She will be like a trapped animal gnawing at its own limb to get out of a trap."

I look at Jessy and try to hear her words but my mind is made up. I will do whatever I can to keep my mother home.

Chapter 21: Commitment

The next couple of days are difficult on the family. I have to give my mom credit for trying. She stops drinking and sobers up. She moves through the house in shock, realizing how much of her life she has lost.

No one in the family talks about what happened when she left four years ago or what she missed. It's as if it never happened. My grandparents are around, maybe a little too much, watching my mom and just being here for her.

I can see the shame on my mother's face sometimes. She doesn't always know how to act, so she just cleans something and that brings a calm over her. I've never seen the house so sparkling.

Mom gets the shakes from her need of alcohol. She becomes despondent and stars having massive mood swings. The first time it happened, I just held her and told her I loved her over and over for almost an hour. It was a test of wills for us both. My mother crying and saying she is sorry and me assuring her everything is all right.

Jessy has been staying with me in my room since I got back. She has not gone home at all because she is afraid she will see her mother or father. She does not want to face her mom about her affair. I am glad as she is a great help to me and the rest of the family during this trying time.

The fact that the Wendigo is getting closer every day is gnawing at me. I need to be in the woods setting up traps but instead I'm baby-sitting my mom. By the third day, I know I've little choice but to get to work.

I consider talking to my dad about the situation but he is already overwhelmed. I decide to confide in my grandfathers. They know this area at least as well as I do if not better, and they already know about the Wendigo and me.

My two grandfathers, Jubal and Amos go out into the woods with me behind my dad's house. We stop in a small clearing we have made into a kind of meeting area over the years. There are several fallen logs that have been positioned and shaped to be comfortable benches and seats around a fire pit.

"The Wendigo is coming here," I let that statement linger in the air for a moment before continuing on. "It is my plan to make a trap for it. The spirits told me that the Wendigo is a spirit of the air and would best be trapped in the earth. I was thinking of using the old hill mine on your property, Amos. If I could get the Wendigo in the mine, I could collapse the entrance and trap it. What do you think?"

"Caleb knows of the mine. Would he not avoid a place he could be trapped?" Jubal asks, scanning the distance as if he can see the Wendigo coming.

Amos speaks before I can. "The malevolent Wendigo spirit knows what Caleb knows, this seems to be true. The Wendigo wants you, Logan. The Wendigo is full of hate and envy of you specifically. You must use this to goad it into entering the mine. Its rage will override any self-preservation it has."

Jubal, intent on what Amos has said, continues. "It's rage may be the key but if you are the bait how do you manage to not get trapped along with the Wendigo? You may find yourself sealed inside a mine shaft with a deadly opponent."

Amos and Jubal sit thinking so I speak. "The possibility of me being trapped with the Wendigo is real. I hope that I can come up with a plan where that does not happen. I've friends close by who will come to my aid and have the means of transporting the Wendigo to a holding facility. My true goal in all this is to eventually free Caleb from the curse of the Wendigo."

"You have to deal with your spirit quest of capturing or killing the Wendigo. The goings-on of your home must be secondary to this," Amos says.

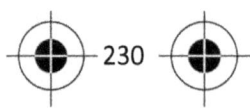

I watch as Jubal nods his head in agreement. "I have already come to the same conclusion, but I needed to hear you say it. Please do whatever you can to keep my home together till I get back," I say.

"We are very proud of you Logan. You have become a fine man, a good son and a great warrior. You keep yourself safe. The family needs your strength," Amos says.

"Thank you grandfathers. I would not be who I am without your guidance and patience."

My grandfathers get up and we walk back to the house. I'm ready to go but I know I need to talk to Jessy first. She is already going through a tough time and I cannot just leave without talking to her. I find her in the midst of the women of my family. She has a forced smile on her face but I can tell she is not enjoying the experience. Right then I realizes I've wronged her. She has no true place here.

My family just sees her as my on and off again girlfriend that they hope I grow out of. I bet if she was a pure blood Seneca they would treat her as one of the family and be pushing us together. Instead, they just tolerate her. She is always an outsider. Even during the last few days when she has helped out so much with my mom, she has still not earned a place among them. I love my grandmothers and I've always seen them as truly good women but their subtle and constant disapproval of Jessy is wrong. I know they are never openly mean or hurtful to Jessy. They are polite and even nice but there is always that hint of "I wish you would go away so our grandson can find a pure blood to marry and give us fine grandchildren" attitude.

Watching Jessy standing now as always to the back, never truly included in the inner circle of the family. Hell, my mother who left for four years sits in a place of honor when Jessy is forced to be on the outside. I love that girl and she is such a comfort to me.

I make a decision more out of anger than anything else. I walk up to the group of my two grandmothers, my mom and Jessy. "Has Jessy told you the good news?"

They all look at me, then to Jessy who seems as surprised as they are. "No. What good news?" my Mom asks.

I hold out my hand for Jessy and she walks over to me so I can put my arm around her. "Jessy and I are engaged. I hope you will all treat her as family, because that is how I already feel about her."

Jessy's knees give out and I have to hold her tight to keep her from falling. I pull her to me and kiss her so the others do not see her shock. My cheeks are wet with Jessy's tears by the end of the kiss. I look into her eyes and can see the love and joy overflowing in her. I know there is no going back now. I made up the

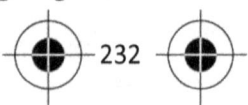

engagement so Jessy would be treated better, but to her it's very real. I know deep in my heart I always knew this day would come. I truly love Jessy. We have grown up together and I look forward to growing old together. Looking at her smile, I know I made the right choice.

I whisper to Jessy. "I hope it's ok that I told my family that I want to marry you."

"Yes…oh God yes, Logan. I love you so much," Jessy whispers through tears of joy.

I feel arms around me and see that my mom has come up to hug Jessy and me. She is crying too, sharing in the moment. Soon my grandmothers join in, hugging and welcoming Jessy to the family. It is the most touching scene I have ever been in. The emotion is so thick in the air, it is overwhelming. By the end of it, I feel drained but happy. I just can't stop smiling.

I want to talk to Jessy but she is swept away by my family to talk of wedding plans. In a way I'm glad to not have to say goodbye. She knows that I'm hunting the Wendigo and that it's hunting me. She does not need to know any more right now. I leave a note on my bed for her.

"To the future Jessy Longstride. I am sorry but I have to go away for a while. I will try to be back at night but that may not be possible. I'm still in the area doing the thing I promised Caleb. Please stay here with our family. Your loving future husband, Logan."

I get the tools, rope and other equipment I will need from the garage and shop before heading out to the mine.

Chapter 22:
The Mine

The mine has three main shafts that crisscross each other. There is the main entrance and a smaller secondary emergency exit down the second shaft. Caleb and I used to play in the mine when we were growing up so we know it's layout well. Yesterday, I probably would have caved in the back exit and made my trap at the main entrance. This plan would make it more likely that the Wendigo would not escape but also has a greater probability of me being trapped inside the mine with it. If that happens it will be a fight to the death between us.

Since today I announced my intentions to marry Jessy, I feel that coming back alive from this fight is more important. Having Jessy waiting for me gives me something wonderful to live for. I need to be more cautious when trapping the Wendigo. I will try to lead the Wendigo into the mine and collapse the front entrance, then make a beeline for the back exit and collapse the exit with the Wendigo on my tail. This is a more complicated plan but should work. I will need to come up with one or two other places in the mine to set traps to collapse other parts of the mine, increasing my chances to trap the Wendigo.

I scout the mine to make sure I remember it correctly. Then I get to work with my chainsaw, felling some trees for lumber to shore up the areas I want to trap. It's harder work than I've done in a long time but the Wendigo's strength flows through me so I work fast. By the end of the first day, I have the front entrance so weakened that if I knock down the two new poles holding up the ceiling, it will collapse.

I work well into the night, preparing the poles and beams I need for the exit and traps in the mine. I finally get in my sleeping bag outside the mine and look up at the stars. Out here in the deep woods with almost no light, the night sky is spectacular. The Alaska sky is even better but it has been awhile since I've just laid and marveled at the vastness of the sky. For some reason I think of White Doe and our visit to the spirit world as I drift off to sleep.

The next day I work on the back exit to the mine. As I'm trying to put in a new beam, the whole thing collapses upon me. I try to leap out of the way but am caught by the torrent of earth and timber. I feel pain all over as my body is brutally hit with hundreds or maybe even thousands of pounds of wood, rock and earth. I hear more than feel bones crack as there is pain all over. The beam I was placing caught at an angle in the shaft and created a small pocket where I lay. My legs are trapped up to my chest but the rest of my body is free.

I tap my watch to call Agent Johansson. The watch seems to be working but I must be too far underground for the signal to get through. After trying my phone and watch multiple times, I get frustrated and hit the panic button. I don't know why its signal should work when the phone did not but I'm in trouble and need help.

There is wetness on my back that I know is blood. I reach around with my arm and the pain is incredible. I manage to feel a huge splinter of wood as big around as a gun barrel sticking into my back. I hope that my quick healing can stop the bleeding so I pull it out. The sharp pain makes me black out.

****

When I wake, there are several earth spirits working to free me. I've no idea how long I have been unconscious. The small earth spirits work steadily getting me free. They soon have the passage by my head open and then work on freeing my legs.

The area in front of me in the mine fills with light. A hand reaches out of the light and I take it. The hand is small, soft and very welcoming. I grab the hand and instantly feel better. The pain washes away from the tips of my fingers all the way to my toes. The hand gently pulls and I can tell the earth elementals are helping to carry me out from under the collapsed tunnel. Soon I am out and in the light filled mineshaft.

There still holding my hand is White Doe. She is smiling at me and I cannot help but smile back. She is wearing a white hide dress that is simpler than the one I saw her in before. Her black hair beautifully frames her oval face. She stares into me with her beautiful dark eyes.

"It is good to see you Logan," she says, sitting down next to me still holding my hand.

She puts my head in her lap and strokes my hair with her free hand. The other hand she keeps in mine. Even when I try to move it she holds on. I think she is soothing my pain with her touch.

I finally look around and see several earth elementals. The light is coming from a large fire elemental that takes up the whole mine shaft behind us. It's more ominous looking than any spirit I've seen so far.

I finally find my tongue. "How did you find me?" I ask, grasping her hand tightly.

"The spirits told me you were in trouble so I came."

"How long have I been here?" I ask, feeling my pain for a second.

"A couple of hours," White Doe says, slowly stroking my hair.

"Thank you for coming."

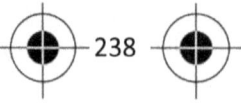

"I was glad to come, I missed you."

"I've thought of you to."

"You really think you can trap the Wendigo in here?"

"I'm going to try…um…how did you know that is what I am going to do?"

"The spirits told me. Ever since we met, I have listened to what they say about Old Broken Nose's chosen one. They call you Spirit Warrior, Mask Hunter and most often simply Longstride. You are the stuff of legend, just at the beginning of your story."

"So you know everything I've been doing since I left you?"

"Not everything but I know where you have been and some of the things you have done. The spirits think you have returned home to gather your strength before the battle with the Wendigo. Is this true?

"Yes…I guess it is. I never really thought about it that way but a lot of my strength comes from my family. I still feel like Caleb is part of my family. I have to help him or put him out of his torment. Either way, I hope this is finished soon."

"Your fight with the Wendigo may end soon but the spirits have just begun complicating your life. You have been chosen by a very powerful spirit of the people. You are destined to be in the middle of grand events the rest of your days. I have learned that being chosen by the spirits is a blessing and a burden."

"You certainly know a lot more about spirits than I do, so I guess you may be right. I feel we choose our own paths in life. Spirits should be there to guide, not control."

"You will not be forced into action by the spirits. In a way, it is all your own choice. But we have both been given great powers. The spirits can show us how those powers can help those we love. When shown such visions, it is hard to walk away from your duty to the people. You cannot even walk away from the duty you feel to one person, Caleb."

"I understand. Did the spirits send you to help me?"

"No. I am not supposed to be here. The people and the spirits wish for me to remain with them in the north. They feel it is too dangerous for me to wander without many warriors. I am held captive by their need of my powers and my duty to the people."

"Then why did you come? Are you going to get in trouble?

"You are my mate. I know I am not the life mate or wife you will choose to be with in the end, but I am still your wife. I love you as a wife loves her husband. I never have experienced this feeling before I met you. I know I am young and may find love again but you are my first love. I came to you as a wife should come to help her husband." White Doe pauses for a moment, smiles at me and then continues. "As for

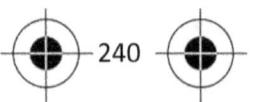

getting in trouble…well I will deal with that when it comes. Sometimes you have to choose the right action no matter what the consequences. I did call this mighty fire elemental to journey with me. He offers me a great amount of protection."

"I'm sorry White Doe. I would never have lain with you if I knew you would feel this way. I do feel a connection to you but our worlds are far apart."

"I know, my Logan. I knew before you lay with me that I would maybe never see you again. It was a choice that I made and do not regret. Let's not speak of it any more right now. What is important now is that you succeed in your hunt of the Wendigo. How may I assist you?"

"I need to get these traps constructed so I can set them off as I sprint by with the Wendigo right on my heels. I would like to make one or two more in the mines along the path between the entrance and the exit so I have more than one chance at trapping the Wendigo."

White Doe looks at the several small earth elementals moving around. "You heard what Longstride needs. Will you help?"

The earth elementals rush into action. Some go deep in the mine to work on the other traps as several work at my feet rebuilding the trap that almost cost me my life. What would have taken me days is taking them minutes. I'm mesmerized by their actions. They seem to be able to make the earth go where they will it. The only part they seem to really have to struggle with is the wooden beams. I guess since wood is not part of earth or rock, they cannot affect it the same way.

I get to my feet with White Doe still holding my hand. I've no pain at all. I actually feel good. I'm at peace and full of a warm feeling that I think is White Doe's love for me. It is strange to truly feel the love of another for you. It is a beautiful thing that I wish I could return. I feel ashamed. I should not have lain with her. She told me the spirits had bid her to lay with me. I wonder why that was? I'm ready to ask her when my watch comes alive with the voice of Agent Johansson.

"Logan, Logan can you hear me? We got your distress signal and are heading out," Agent Johansson says.

I speak into the watch. "It's all right. I'm ok. You don't have to come," I say, watching White Doe's expression change to one of sadness.

"What happened? Report!" Agent Johansson demands.

"It was a cave-in that had me trapped but I am free now. I'm fine."

"Ok, we'll stand down. Keep me updated," Agent Johansson says.

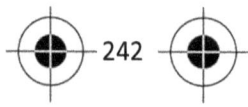

I look at White Doe and realize she knows I've lain with Agent Johansson. White Doe is so innocent to the sexual world that exists outside her woods. I don't know what to say, so I say nothing. I'm surprised when it's White Doe who speaks about it.

"She is not the one, Logan. She would never give you the strength you will need."

"I know. I've always known that deep down."

"Then why lie with her?"

"I guess because I could. She is a beautiful woman. I enjoyed being with her. I'm pretty sure neither of us expected anything more than sex. Neither of us was hurt and we had a good time."

"Neither of you may have been hurt. But what about the one that waits for you in your home. Does it hurt her when you have a good time with other women? Is that what I was to you? A good time?" White Doe says as she lets go of my hand.

Agonizing pain surges through me and I fall to my knees. I know now that White Doe's love was holding back the pain. When she let go of my hand it rushed back.

"Logan you are better than this. I felt it when I joined with you. Be the man I know you can be!" White Doe almost screams at me.

It's difficult with all the pain but I look up at her. Her face is filled with tears. She reaches down to me and places her hand on my head. I feel the torment start to wash away. Even now her love is true and calming to me.

"I wanted to spend time with you. I wanted this time with you, husband. I was going to try to lay with you again tonight and heal you slowly. But I can see that is not going to happen now. To me you will always be more than just a good time. You should not hurt those who love you Logan."

She pushes her hand hard against my head and a spike of pain as I've never felt shoots through me. I struggle against the torture but cannot keep from passing out.

Chapter 23: Trust

I'm in the woods hunting. I know this place. It's my Aunt and Uncle Longstride's land. I used to play in these woods as a child. Just down that hill is their cabin. My Aunt Tammy, Uncle Ben and their daughter Ruby live here. Over to my left I can smell the sweet water of the swimming lake. This place has so many happy memories for me.

I catch the scents of the cabin. Lingering smells of cooked meat, fresh baked bread and corn. Smoke from the chimney. The musty smell of Toby and Jake, the two hound dogs. And the sweet smell of my prey.

I run down the hill, almost walking on the wind. I can see the cabin now. It's as I remembered it even though I've not been here for a couple years. A wide porch runs all around it. On the side is the porch swing that we broke twice from swinging too high on it.

The whimpering of the dogs from under the porch drifts to my ears. I wonder why they do not come out to greet me. We always had a good time playing together. They really liked it when I threw sticks into the lake for them to fetch.

I'm starving and anxious to eat. I walk up to the cabin door and go in. One thing that has not changed is no one locks their door out here in the woods. I walk through the dark house. My aunt and uncle should be in their room in the back. I stalk down the hall as if I am hunting prey. I slowly open the door and see my aunt and uncle gently sleeping. Maybe I should come back. But I'm so hungry. I have to eat.

I dive upon my uncle ripping into his flesh with my claws. My aunt screams and I hear a distant scream that must be from my sweet cousin upstairs.

****

I awake thrashing upon the dirt of the cave. I was just inside the Wendigo. It's here. Well a couple hours from here to the north. Damn, I never thought about it going after Aunt Tammy and Uncle Ben. Who else will it attack before making its way to my house? Damn it! I should have thought this through better.

I physically feel good and all my wounds are healed. I remember White Doe and look around but she is nowhere to be found. By my watch, I've only been out a couple of hours. I walk the mine and see that the earth elementals finished the traps for me. I head back home and call Agent Johansson on the way.

"The Wendigo is about a hundred miles to the north. I expect contact in the next twenty four hours."

"I understand and will stand by. Keep me up to date," Agent Johansson says.

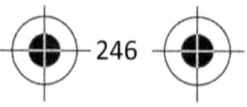 246

It's around ten when I pull into the house. Even from the driveway, I can hear the yelling. I slowly walk to the house trying to make out what all the commotion is about. My mom seems to be freaking out because she overcooked the meatloaf. God I don't know if I can handle this after the day I've had. I consider just getting back in my car and driving away, but this is my family. They are what I'm fighting for. No matter how emotionally drained I feel I'm the one that brought mom home and I need to do what I can. Resolved to face the situation I go in.

"And where the hell have you been? You didn't even say goodbye and now the meatloaf is ruined," my Mom screams at me as I walk in the door.

"Nice to see you too, mom," I say evenly as I take off my jacket.

"Don't use that tone with me. I'm your mother, damn it," she screams.

"Then start acting like it. Who cares if the meatloaf is ruined or I went out. We can eat something else and I came back and am here now. Everything is fine," I say calmly as I walk over to her.

"FINE! How can anything ever be fine again? I need a damn drink," my Mom yells as she frantically looks around as if there should be a bottle of booze in sight.

I see Faith in the corner of the room sitting on a chair. Her knees are pulled up to her chest and her arms are wrapped around them. She is slowly rocking back and forth in her chair. I go over to her and put my arm around her.

"Where are you going? Oh, I see. You are like all the rest. You like Faith best," my Mom screams as she throws a candlestick at me, which hits me in the back.

"She's going to leave again, isn't she?" Faith whispers to me through sobs. I can't tell if this would make her happy or sad.

"No she's not," I say with a resolve that makes Faith look at me wide eyed.

I get up and walk right at my mother. I can see fear in her eyes as she sees the resolve in mine. She looks away and knows she has gone too far. She seems strangely calm as if she is used to pushing too far and being manhandled because of it. I think she strangely welcomes the beating she thinks I'm going to give her because it is familiar. What she can't handle is the daily life of being a mother and wife.

Jessy gets in my way as I am marching to my mom. "Logan, she is your mom," she says as she puts her hand on my arm.

Both sets of grandparents, my dad, Faith and Jessy are all watching me to see what I'm going to do. I'm not as much angry as I am just tired of my mom acting like a child. I stand there seething with only Jessy between my mom and me.

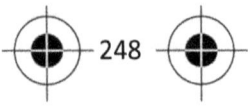

"We are all going outside," I command, more than say.

I look down at Jessy. "Can you bring Faith outside with you…please?"

Her eyes are unsure but she moves to go get Faith. I take my mom's hand in mine. "Let's go outside, mother," is all I say, as I half-lead and half-pull her outside.

I walk with my mom down upon the grass. The others congregate on the porch. I take in a deep breath and begin.

"Mother, this is your family. We stuck together and survived you leaving." My mom starts to speak but my quick glance and a strong squeeze of her hand stops her. "You need to decide if you want to be part of our family or not. If you stay, you need to act like a mother and a wife. If you go, you need to go far so we never have to see you again. I know you feel your problems are too big and you can never make up for all the time you lost. We are not asking for that. We just want you to be with us. We all forgive you. You have to forgive yourself as well."

"Since you have been gone many things have changed. Faith has become a fine young lady. She needs a mother in the house. I have graduated with a degree in Archaeology. And there are secret things not all here know. You feel your problems are so huge and overwhelming, but they are nothing compared to what is going on involving the whole family."

"I assume you know Caleb died. Well, he did not die. He was trapped in a cabin with some other men without food. He became a cannibal to survive and was possessed by a Wendigo spirit."

My mom looks at me like I'm crazy, shaking her head. "Oh it gets better. I fought with the Wendigo and almost died." I pull off my shirt and show everyone the massive scare of the Wendigo claws on my left shoulder. My mom touches the scar in disbelief, her hand shaking.

"As I wavered near death, I had a vision of Old Broken Nose. He told me to make a mask of the Wendigo to gain its power. When I returned home, I did this. I've since then encountered the Wendigo a couple times in vicious battle. Even now the Wendigo is hunting all of us. It will come home, where it feels safe, to feast on the flesh of man." Faith gasps, and I wonder if I was right to include her in this.

"I've set traps for the Wendigo and go to face it once again. I fight for you, for my family. If I should fall, you all need to leave and not come back until the killing stops."

Only my grandfathers and dad are somewhat calm. All the women are on edge. My mom is the most skeptical, but I can see she at least is listening.

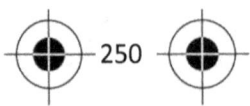

"A nice tale to scare me into behaving, but that is all it is," my Mom says. "Prove it."

"I shouldn't have to prove it. You are my family and know me. I have grown into a man of my word and that should be good enough."

"I believe you brother, even though it scares me to death," Faith says.

"I believe you Logan," Jessy says.

My grandfathers and father next say they believe me, then my grandmothers chime in. Everyone turns to look at my mom.

"Logan I am trying. I really am but I'm just no good anymore. You should give up on me and let me go," my Mom says and she turns away from me.

"That is the first real truth I've heard you say since you came home. But we have not given up on you. It's you who has given up on yourself, on us. Do you believe my story?" I ask.

"I'm sorry, Logan, but no," she says, crossing her arms to hug herself.

"Why? Why can't you just take my word?"

"I've seen too much from the bottom of a bottle to believe in anything ever again," she laughs bitterly.

"Even yourself? Or your son?"

"Yep, I'm just no good. There are no spirits or monsters except those that live inside us. I've seen my internal devil destroy my life."

"What if there were spirits and monsters? If I can prove to you what I say is true and real, would that give you hope that maybe even you can change. If something so fantastic is real then wouldn't it be a little thing to believe in yourself again."

"It doesn't matter, they are not real."

"Mother, I'm making you a deal. If I can prove my words, I want your promise that you will stay and try every day to believe in yourself and be a good mother to Faith and me and a wife to your husband. If I cannot convince you, then I will never come after you again and all I ask is you move far away so we do not have to see you destroy yourself. You are always welcome to come back home but we'll not seek you out or force you to come home. Do we have a deal?" I say, holding out my hand so we can shake on it.

"Sure Logan, whatever," she says holding out her hand, but I do not take it.

"No Mother, this is not a whatever situation. This is a life changing moment for you. Do you swear to stand by this deal on the lives of your family? I want your word, Mother."

My mother looks at me and sees that I am deadly serious. I think for the first time she is actually afraid she may lose this bet. I think part of her wants to. It would be the harder road to stay with the family and she chose to run away last time to the bottom of a bottle when my dad got hurt.

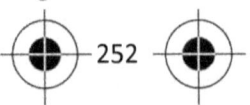

"Ok Logan I swear on the lives of my family that I will abide by our deal," my Mom says and we shake on it.

"As I said, I made a mask to gain the powers of the Wendigo. The Wendigo is fast," I say as I race around the yard and porch in a blur I move so fast. My grandmothers and mom gasp at the sight of me. Faith is more in awe and does not seem afraid at all. Jess is sitting beside her with a look of pride on her face.

"The Wendigo can leap great distances," I say, as I leap to the roof of the house and then onto a branch almost forty feet away. More gasps of disbelief come from my mom and grandmothers. Faith claps and stands on her chair so she can see better.

"The Wendigo is strong," I go over to my car and pick the front of it off the ground.

"I can also heal very fast. I will prove it if you want," I say pulling out Enuk's knife.

"No Logan...I believe you...my son," my Mom says and she holds her arms out. I walk over to her and she hugs me.

"You tricked me," she whispers in my ear.

"You should have believed me. Welcome home, Mom."

"I'm glad to be home, Logan. Thanks for not giving up on me," my Mom whispers as she holds me tight.

I know she won't change overnight but this is a good start. I hope she can make it.

Chapter 24: Jessy is Gone

The next day I make sure the whole family comes to the house to stay together until this is all over. It gets pretty crowded and I give up my bedroom for my grandparents. Jessy and I are sleeping on an air mattress in the basement.

With everyone settled, I go out into the woods. I circle the house in constantly in widening circles trying to catch the scent of the Wendigo. Around noon, I've still not picked anything up. I wonder if I have missed something. The thought gnaws at me so I head home but everything is quiet. I have lunch and try to be as upbeat as possible. Everyone is on edge and part of me wishes I had not told them about the Wendigo. The funny thing is my mom is doing really well. She looks at me with eyes filled with pride for the man I have become.

I head back out to the woods to repeat my search midafternoon. Around seven, I head back to the house. I want to be around so everyone will feel a little safer before bed. My dad greets me at the door.

"Jessy is gone," my dad says before I even open the screen door. "Her dad has been arrested by the sheriff. She went to go try and get him out of jail."

I stand there trying to think of what to do. I want to go get her but that would leave my family unprotected. She did go into town, so should be safe. She should have just left her father in jail. That is probably one of the safest places for him right now.

I call Jessy but no answer. I decide to call Agent Johansson. "Just reporting in. I expect contact any time now."

"Understood. Be safe Logan," Agent Johansson says.

I'm starting to feel the tension and begin to second-guess my motives here. I hope that in trying to save Caleb, I haven't condemned my family. If the trap works or not, this has to end. If I fail in capturing the Wendigo, it has to be destroyed. I cannot play this game of cat and mouse anymore. Too many people are dying. It ends here.

I call Jessy again but still no answer. I'm pacing through the house holding my phone when my Grandfather Amos comes up to me. "You are scaring everyone. Calm down," Amos quietly tells me.

I look around and see that everyone is watching me. I wanted to keep everyone calm but I've done the opposite. Damn you Jessy. Why did you have to leave?

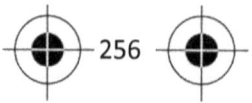

I try to smile and calm down but I know it's no good. I tell everyone I'm going to look around outside. I search around the house and finally catch the scent of the Wendigo. I feel strangely relieved to know the Wendigo is close. It's funny how the waiting is always the worst. I might die fighting the Wendigo but the waiting is tearing me up inside.

I follow the scent which leads away from the house. I backtrack back to the house just to make sure but I'm right. It never made it all the way to the house. It stopped near the road as it was coming toward the house. Something happened right here that made it go away from the house and follow the road. Then it hits me. The Wendigo must have seen or smelled Jessy as she drove by on her way to town. The Wendigo is hunting Jessy. Caleb knew Jessy was my girl and now he wants to take her from me. I run down the road follow the Wendigo scent as fast as I can go. I'm coming, Jessy.

When I'm almost to town, I hear the squeal of brakes and a crashing of metal. I come around a bend in time to see the Wendigo pulling Jessy out of her smashed up car. I charge right at them and pull Enuk's knife out. I slam into the Wendigo, driving the knife deep into it's back. Jessy lets out an audible sound of pain as the Wendigo drops her.

I wrestle the Wendigo away from Jessy and we face each other. Jessy is hurt but conscious. She watches as the Wendigo and I sidestep in a circle preparing for battle. The gaunt body of Caleb is standing before me, naked and ashen white. His black eyes show no sign of the Caleb I knew. All there is in this beast right now is the Wendigo. I don't know if I could kill Caleb but I can kill the Wendigo, especially to protect Jessy.

All the sudden, the Wendigo leaps at me. I sidestep and slash upwards with my knife. I cut an insignificant gash in the Wendigo's leg. As I turn to face the Wendigo, I realize the leap was not meant so much to attack me as a way to get closer to Jessy. The Wendigo is upon Jessy before I can even act. Its clawed hand rises in the air to give the killing blow. It's dead eyes look back at me and I see the thing smile at me. It wants me to watch it kill the woman I love. It's getting pleasure from tormenting me. I knew this was personal but I didn't know how personal until this moment.

I do the only thing I can think of. I scream, "CALEB, STOP" and rush at him. The eyes of the Wendigo start to clear and it's hand wavers in the air. It only lasts a split second but it's enough time for me to cover the ground between us and get my body in the way of its claws. I take the blow meant for Jessy on my right side. Pain shoots through me and I can feel the wetness of blood on my side. I push the Wendigo with all my might away from Jessy.

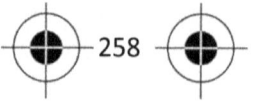

The Wendigo bears its pointed teeth at me and I realize that right now Jessy is the best bait for my trap. I hate to put her through this. I've no idea how hurt she is but she is my best hope of trapping the Wendigo. I pick her up and run into the woods with the Wendigo right on my heels. I head straight for the mine but it's several miles away. I know where I'm going so that gives me a slight edge in our race. But I'm hurt and every stride brings bolts of pain and pumps out more of my blood.

The pain gets to me and I miss a jump. I roll upon the ground, spilling Jessy several feet away. She screams in pain from the impact and I know she must have been hurt worse that I thought from the car crash. I struggle to my feet and try to get to Jessy but the Wendigo slams me into a tree before I can make it. It takes me a moment to get my breath, a moment I do not have.

The Wendigo is between me and Jessy just waiting for me to see what it has planned for my love. Well I'm not finished yet. I draw Enuk's knife and stand tall. I fight the pain back and walk at the Wendigo. It howls it's unearthly call and charges me. We slash at each other and I manage to make a savage gash down it's right arm. I come out of the exchange mostly unhurt. The Wendigo's useless right arm dangles limp. It howls again and comes at me. I've a strange calmness over me right now. I attack as if this battle is for my life, which it may very well be. I cut into the Wendigo's chest leaving a huge gash. The Wendigo manages to catch me with its left arm in my right shoulder. It is a bad wound and will make fighting difficult for me.

As the Wendigo reels from its wounds, I grab Jessy and head off toward the mine. I notice that the Wendigo is not following so I decide to goad it. "Caleb...oh...Caleb...I've got Jessy...come and get her if you can...come on Caleb...Caleb."

I hear the roar of the howling windy cry of the Wendigo and I know my plan worked. I press on toward the mine with the Wendigo closing in behind me.

I slow just a little as I near the mine. I want the Wendigo to be right on my heels when I set the trap. I know that no matter what happens, this ends here and now so I hit the panic button on my watch. Agent Johansson and the Hounds will be heading out to help me now. They should be here in the next ten minutes, but that is an eternity when faced with an enemy like the Wendigo. I know this is up to me.

I enter the mine with the Wendigo right behind me. I hit the board that triggers the trap and hear the crash of earth and rock behind me. I've no time to look back so press on as fast as I can. I get to the next trap set up by the earth elementals and set it off. Tons of earth floods the passage behind me but I do not

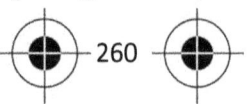

stop. I keep running and can tell the Wendigo is still coming. I hit the next trap and still the Wendigo makes it through. I have to get ahead of the Wendigo enough to catch it in the avalanche of earth.

Jessy is moaning on my back and I know she must be in bad shape. But probably in her best condition, it would be punishing to be carried at these speeds. I decide I have to risk hurting Jessy even more. At the back entrance of the mine, I push Jessy out and spin to meet the Wendigo. It crashes into me and we roll upon the earth pounding into each other. Each blow of the beast nearly shatters my bones. I know they would easily break if I didn't have the resilience of the Wendigo given to me when I made my mask.

I manage to get to my feet and concentrate on pushing the Wendigo deep into the mine so I can set off the trap. I slice at the Wendigo driving it back but still it is not enough. I'm taking too much damage and not getting anywhere. I risk moving way too close and just shove the Wendigo as hard as I can. My attack has the desired effect but I take a vicious gash to my chest in return. I leap out of the mine, catching the trap trigger as I soar past it. I hear the wail of the Wendigo, "WaaEee," muffled by the torrent of tons of earth. Finally, I've trapped the Wendigo.

I contact Agent Johansson. "I've trapped the Wendigo in a mine shaft. I'm hurt and with a friend who is very hurt."

"Understood. We'll be on site in a couple minutes," Agent Johansson says.

I move to Jessy and I'm thankful to see she is still breathing. I look her over and from the bruising on her stomach and back, I think she has several broken ribs. She looks up at me and smiles. I smile back at her.

"I love you Jessy," I say, kissing her forehead.

She smiles more and tears fall out of the sides of her eyes. I can tell she is really in pain. "Help is on the way. You are going to be ok," I promise Jessy.

Soon the helicopter is overhead. Below it is dangling the huge thick holding container. I have to move Jessy and talk to the pilot to get the container into place at the exit to the mine. It takes a couple of tries but soon is in place. The cables are dropped and the chopper lands a short way away in a clearing. Two of the Hounds have a stretcher for Jessy. I help get her on it and say my goodbyes.

"I want her taken to the hospital right now," I tell Agent Johansson.

"Our first priority is the Wendigo," Agent Johansson says.

"You take her to the hospital right now. It will only take two of the Hounds. The rest of us can get

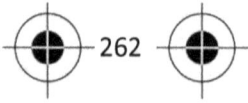

ready for the transfer." I see indecision in Agent Johansson so I continue. "Please...she is important to me."

Agent Johansson looks at me and then nods. With Jessy heading off to the hospital, I get to work on figuring out how we are going to get the Wendigo into the black box of a containment cell.

Agent Johansson stops me and calls over a Hound. "Logan you are hurt. Let's at least stop the bleeding. We don't need you killing yourself after your first successful capture."

The Hound goes to work bandaging me up. I still have the pain but have stopped loosing blood.

The oubliette, as the Hounds call the containment cell is designed with this situation in mind. It's capable of drilling into the dirt and extending a reinforced shaft into the hole it has drilled out. One of the Hounds gets on the controls and the drilling starts. Ten minutes later the shaft is extended fifty feet and the camera shows we have hit the open passage inside the mine. We can see the Wendigo through the video watching the shaft.

"Logan, you need to get it into the shaft. If we can do that, the shaft end will be shut and the Wendigo will be caught. The shaft will then slowly collapse and the Wendigo will be forced to retreat into the oubliette. You can talk to it through this mic here," Agent Johansson says.

"Caleb...come and get me Caleb," I say into the mic.

The Wendigo turns and stares at the shaft where my voice is coming from. It seems to hesitate but I call for it again and it enters the shaft. The end is sealed and the shaft is retracted. We have caught the Wendigo.

Agent Johansson pats me on the shoulder, which sends surges of pain through me. "Sorry, Logan. Well anyway, that is a good job done. We will take the Wendigo back to base. I figure you want a couple of days to recuperate."

"Yeah, I want to spend time with my family. I'll be in touch."

"See ya, Logan," Agent Johansson says as she turns and starts barking orders at the Hounds.

Chapter 25:
Jessy Time

I walk into the woods towards the hospital. I call my house and arrange for my grandfather Amos to meet me at the hospital with a change of clothes, as mine are all torn and covered in blood.

I soon am jogging towards the hospital even though I hurt all over. I arrive at the hospital and meet Amos. I can tell I must look pretty bad from the expression on his face. I change and head in to find out where Jessy is. I tell them I'm her husband so they will let me see her. When I start to get the run around, I pull out my FBI badge and get to see her right away. I guess a badge can come in handy.

Jessy has five broken ribs, a concussion and a lot of bruising. She also has a pretty deep five-fingered claw mark on her upper right thigh. It will become a scar that will remind her of this night forever.

I sit with Jessy all night and the next day until she wakes up. The doctor said it would be good for me to talk to her while she sleeps. I find a romance novel about a young woman who falls in love with her doctor that I read aloud to her. It has some heaving breast scenes but at least gives me something to do.

"Oh doctor! You are all the medicine I need. Give it to me," Karen said, breathless from his manly embrace.

Doctor Drake crushes Karen's body into his as their lips meet. Their tongues dance in a loving embrace. Their hands roam each other's body caressing. Soon Drake has undone Karen's blouse revealing her ample breasts still trapped in their scarlet red cage. Drake kisses the top of each breast, sending shivers down Karen's spine.

"What the hell are you reading?" Jessy asks.

I look up to see Jessy finally has her eyes open and is awake. I'm not sure how long she has been awake. She is grinning at me reading the steamy romance to her. I smile back and lean over to give her a light kiss. "It's about time you wake up, sleepy head."

"What happened?"

She tries to sit up but the pain makes her reconsider and she lays back. I tell her pretty much all of what happened.

"So it's over?"

"For now. I want to free Caleb from the Wendigo spirit. To do that, I have to find artifacts and I'm not sure where to start. My grandfathers are looking into it, I will use my new government contacts and I hope the spirits will help. I've a feeling that it's not

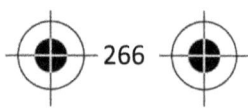

something that will happen overnight. For now, I just want to have some time, some Jessy time."

"I think Jessy time will consist of you waiting on me hand and foot until I can manage to move," Jessy laughs, but abruptly stops as it hurts way too much.

"Your wish is my command," I grin at her.

Over the next two weeks, I take Jessy home to my house and take care of her. My mother is not perfect but she stays and for now that seems to be the important thing. Jessy heals fast but is still very sore and slow getting around. We just all try to figure out how to live together. I know that if I stay here, I will need my own place but right now, this is definitely my home.

****

PAIN...ALL THERE IS, IS PAIN! My body tenses over and over as the electricity surges through me. The pain is beyond imagination. Why are they doing this to me? Then it stops and my body falls limp. My muscles are sore from being constantly stimulated by the electricity over and over.

"Subject Caleb still shows no signs of losing consciousness to electrical assault. We have used amounts that would kill ten men and yet it fights through the pain. I didn't believe it possible."

"Healing tests all show it has an incredibly fast regeneration rate. Even the most grievous wounds are fully healed in twenty-four hours. It seems to also be able to continue fighting through the pain it receives. So far, blood and tissue samples have not shown any possibilities for replication."

"It is thought by some that the abilities of this Wendigo are purely from a supernatural spirit residing inside the human host. This query of research will be explored next," Horst Stecher head of research for the HEL facility says.

I'm so hungry. I want to eat him to stop the pain in my gut. I want to eat them all. I look at my right arm where the leather strap is around my wrist. I twist my thumb so far back it breaks. But now my claw can reach the strap. I work at the strap. Cutting it more with every passing moment.

One of the white coats comes over to reposition the electric probes in my body. As he pulls one out and moves it to another position on my chest, I finish cutting the strap. I grab him and bring his sweet meat into my mouth. I hear Horst Stecher in the background.

"No, he's already dead. Let's watch how it feeds."

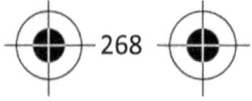 268

****

I awake with a start in my bed next to Jessy. I know I was just the Wendigo. I can feel phantom pain in my own muscles from the electric shock. How could they do that to Caleb? This was not part of my deal with them. Damn it! I should have known better than to trust people who work in a place called HEL.

I don't know what I'm going to do, but I know there will be a reckoning.

PLEASE WRITE A REVIEW!
A review is the best way you can help the author. Please take a second to go back to where you downloaded or bought this book and write a review. There are quick links to all the places this book is sold at LucasMcWilliams.com/books

Thank you so much for your help in spreading the word about my book!
Lucas

Books by Lucas McWilliams
Savage Summer
Eternal Hunt
Eternal Lies
Wielders – Children's Chapter Books

About the Author

 Lucas McWilliams has been writing books for years but just started publishing them. He spends a lot of his time sitting in front of the computer with his oldest daughter writing stories that they come up with together.

Lucas lives with his family on a hilltop close to the Kentucky River Palisades. His loving family includes Lucas' wife, the local librarian, three wonderfully silly daughters, several outdoor cats and their dog Peanut.

You can contact him at
www.Wielders.us
www.LucasMcWilliams.com

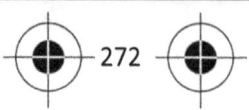

Savage Summer

Set in contemporary Seattle, *SAVAGE SUMMER* is a YA novel that is a supernatural thriller as well as a love story.

Seventeen-year-old Duncan is pretty sure he died recently in the car crash that killed his foster mother. His life really gets complicated when he is thrust into a new foster home, a new high school, falls in love with Amber, the hottest redhead in school, joins her rock band Savage Summer and develops a disturbing thirst for blood.

The band, Savage Summer, gets a gig at a local club, Eros, which turns out to be a haven for vampires. Duncan is forced to protect his new girlfriend Amber and the rest of the band from hungry bloodsuckers and the seductive tunes of Zeal, the vampire rock star.

Meanwhile the ruler of the city's vampires, Sapphire, is trying to seduce Duncan. But all Duncan is really interested in is trying to be a normal kid who feels he has finally found a family with Amber and Savage Summer. Duncan struggles with his love for Amber versus the realization she might be safer if he just walked away.

Eternal Lies
Lucas McWilliams

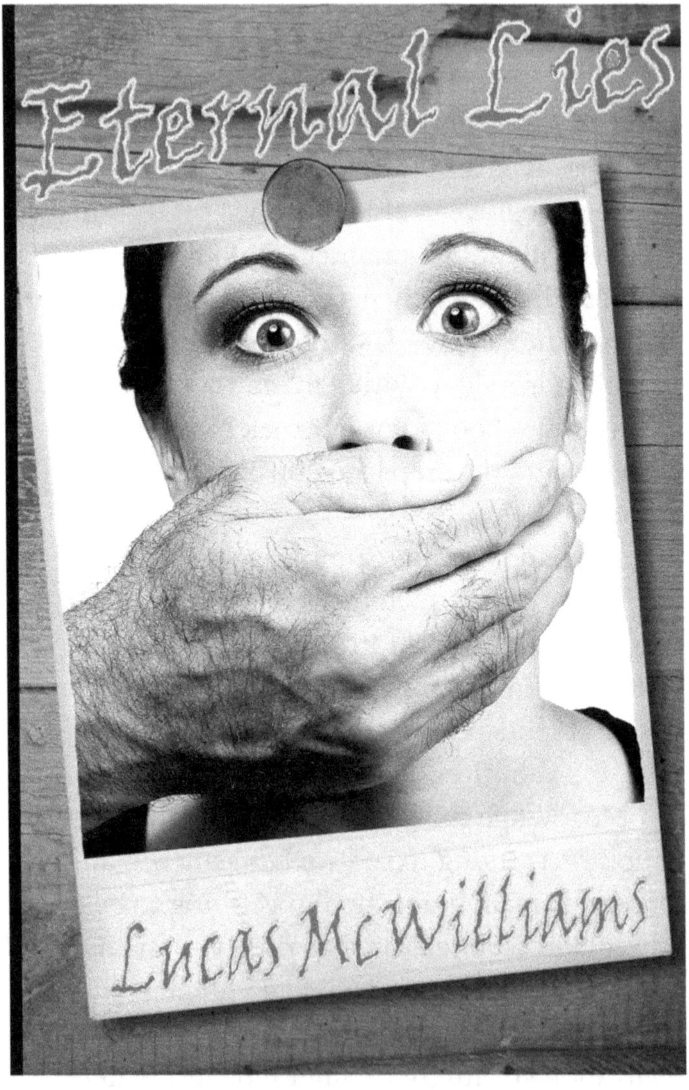

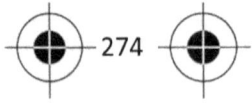

Eternal Lies: Becket Chronicles

ETERNAL LIES is a supernatural thriller as well as a love story.

Unknown to Becket, she was destined to join her old Italian family business of working for the patriarch Antal Degano, an ancient vampire. But all that changed when she encountered a six-year-old bloodsucker who wants Becket to replace her long dead mommy.

Becket joins a secret organization that investigates supernatural creatures to try to empower herself to fight Lilly, the child vampire hellion hunting her. Lilly's pursuit causes her to leave her old life, join the FBI, become a special agent but she falls in love along the way.

Becket has always been special. She inherited an enhanced sense that gives her an edge and the ability to see flashes of the past related to objects she touches. With these gifts and her new training, she turns the tables on Lilly. The hunted becomes the hunter and the only problem is no one told Lilly.

Chapter Books by father-daughter team Lucas and Sophia McWilliams

Wielders #1 The Journey Begins
Wielders #2 First Battle
Wielders #3 The Hunter
Wielders #4 Silver Town Championship
Wielders #5 Lost Friend
And look for more coming out soon!
www.Wielders.us
www.LucasMcWilliams.com

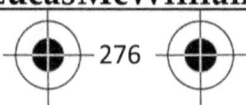

www.ingramcontent.com/pod-product-compliance
Lightning Source LLC
Chambersburg PA
CBHW071125170626
46809CB00002B/500